This is thy hour O Soul, thy free flight into the wordless . . .
pondering the themes thou lovest best,
Night, sleep, death and the stars.

A chill flutters over my skin. Walt Whitman. I saw that poem in the book Alex was cataloging yesterday. Oh God. Please don't let him be the desk poet. I wanted it to be someone mysterious and dark and moody. Anybody but mysterious and dark and moody Alex Hammond.

I erase the words. We both ponder the same dark themes, apparently. I can't help but shiver. It would be so easy to be friends with Alex. In theory, at least. But it would also be wrong. He dated my sister. Was a Bad Influence on my sister. Probably copying the moody poetry as his own way of mourning. I decide not to write anything back. This needs to stop.

DREAMING OF ANTIGONE

Robin Bridges

KENSINGTON BOOKS
www.kensingtonbooks.com

KENSINGTON BOOKS are published by

Kensington Publishing Corp.
119 West 40th Street
New York, NY 10018

Copyright © 2016 by Robin Bridges

All Kensington titles, imprints, and distributed lines are available at special quantity discounts for bulk purchases for sales promotion, premiums, fundraising, educational, or institutional use.

Special book excerpts or customized printings can also be created to fit specific needs. For details, write or phone the office of the Kensington Sales Manager: Kensington Publishing Corp., 119 West 40th Street, New York, NY 10018. Attn. Sales Department. Phone: 1-800-221-2647.

Kensington and the K logo Reg. U.S. Pat. & TM Off.

eISBN-13: 978-1-4967-0355-2
eISBN-10: 1-4967-0355-3
First Kensington Electronic Edition: April 2016

ISBN-13: 978-1-4967-0354-5
ISBN-10: 1-4967-0354-5
First Kensington Trade Paperback Printing: April 2016

10 9 8 7 6 5 4 3 2 1

Printed in the United States of America

For Parham,
A magic moment I remember:
I raised my eyes and you were there.

Acknowledgments

Andria's story has been brewing in the back of my mind ever since I read the play *Antigone* in college, and I have so many souls to thank for their support and inspiration as a vague idea based on a Greek tragedy evolved over the years into a love story.

Merci beaucoup to all of my friends in the YA writing community for your encouragement, especially to Amanda K. Morgan, who read the earliest-ever draft of *DOA* almost ten years ago and became Alex's first fan, and also to Rebecca Phillips, who read one of the very last drafts.

Everlasting thanks to Ethan Ellenberg, the best agent ever, and to my wonderful editor, Alicia Condon, as well as everyone else at Kensington who has helped bring Andria's story to life. Especially for the beautiful starry cover that made me cry. I sincerely hope I didn't drive my copy editor insane with the abundance of poetry in these pages.

Most of all, thank you to Jessica McCabe for being there for me when I was having a Category 5 manuscript crisis. You. Are. My. Hero. And to the rest of my Pediatrics night nurses: Fran, Hannah, Nancy, Mary, Maddy, Darcy, Meghan, and Janell— no matter where (or when) you work now, all of you are still my night crew and I want to thank you for the caffeine and camaraderie over the years. You are all stellar!

And finally, a heartwarming thanks to all YA book lovers, especially those who take the time to blog about the books they love. You are my kind of people. If you're ever in the hospital and can't sleep, you're welcome to stop by the Peds nursing station and chat about books with my night crew. The coffeepot is always full.

CHAPTER 1

Fourteen Days

I see my sister walking through the woods behind our house in late autumn. The trees are bare and everything smells of dead leaves and damp earth. She doesn't look at me, but I know her eyes are an unnatural pale, pale blue. Like the color of her ancient Volkswagen.

She turns her face to me, her movements jerky and stiff. Discordant. Her long slender limbs look mismatched, like they've been sewn on to a rag doll. As her eyes meet mine, she doesn't smile but mouths one word.

"Andria."

I wake up in a cold sweat, with the scent of decayed leaves still lingering on my skin. My heart knocks wildly up against my ribs, so hard I think it might burst out of my chest, and I know. My sister still blames me for her death.

It will be hours before my alarm goes off, but I haven't needed it in months. The nightmares of Iris have been waking me up every night since she died. I can't go back to sleep now. I might as well go out and check the telescope.

I'm quiet, even though I know my mom and stepdad won't hear me sneak out of the house. My stepdad wears a monstrous breathing machine over his face every night to prevent sleep apnea. Mom worries that he will stop breathing. She also worries that I'll have a seizure and swallow my own tongue. She worries about all sorts of things. Funny she never worried about Iris overdosing on heroin.

We live in a sleepy cul-de-sac with no street light in one of Athens's historic neighborhoods. There are lots of trees looming everywhere, but from our back deck, I have a clear view of the northern sky. Especially when the moon has already set. I sneak outside in my robe and slippers and turn the back porch light off. The night is clear and chilly. A perfect black sky dusted with stars. And Jupiter, cuddling up close to Cygnus and Vega. Always a ladies' man, that Jupiter.

I uncover the lens on my telescope, ignoring how cold the metal feels against my skin. My breath spirals out visibly, and there's frost on the grass in the yard, but there's nowhere I'd rather be. The stars are calling me. I'd like to think that Iris is up there somewhere. Finally at peace. I think she'd like the Butterfly Nebula. Four thousand light-years away, it hangs out in the tail of Scorpius.

Our dark street is something else that causes my mother to worry endlessly. She has written letters to city councilmen and stands up in every single homeowner's association meeting, demanding a street light for Azalea Cove. None of the other neighbors really seem to care, though.

The property directly behind ours has been vacant for over a year, which makes me happy, since the old couple that used to live there had floodlights with a magnitude brighter than the sun. Now I can actually see the stars when I step out onto the deck at night.

"Andria? What are you doing out there?" My mother's sleepy voice sounds from the back door. "You'll catch your death of cold."

She's really obsessing over my death now. She's not just saying that.

I put the lens cap back on and say good-bye to Jupiter in my head, before following Mom back inside.

It's still dark, and the clock on the microwave says it's only 4:50. But Mom is already turning on the coffeemaker. "Don't forget to take your meds," she says, sliding the pill bottle across the counter toward me.

I don't let her see me roll my eyes. "I'll take them with breakfast. In another hour or two." Maybe I can get some studying in first. If she doesn't follow me to my room to talk.

"That's fine. I'll have pancakes and sausage waiting for you when you're ready." I hear her set the frying pan on top of the burner as I head down the hallway. She still fixes a full, well-balanced breakfast for me and my stepdad every morning before going to work. Every. Single. Morning.

Ever since Iris's death, I've been smothered with maternal attention.

No, that's not right.

I've always been smothered. Since I had my first seizure when I was three hours old, I've been the one Mom hovered over and coddled. Iris got to be free and do pretty much whatever she wanted.

In my room I open my closet, trying to decide what to wear to school. Everything hanging up is black. Like my hair. And my fingernails and toenails. I've spent all of my life trying to be cooler than my sister, and failing utterly.

More than once in the past months, I've crept into Iris's

room, wishing she was still here, still being cooler than me. Mom has started several times to box stuff up and pack my sister's things away. But she never gets very far. None of us are ready to move on.

I run my fingers over the jewel-colored sweaters and sassy little sundresses in Iris's closet, knowing I can't ever be the blazing star that she was. I'm still just a cold, dark satellite orbiting a star that went supernova.

This is where my stepdad finds me, sitting on the floor in my sister's closet.

"Andria? What are you doing?" He sounds congested, his voice still hoarse from sleep.

"Looking for one of my shirts. I think she borrowed it." We both know this is a lie. Iris teased me about my emo wardrobe. The only time she borrowed one of my black sweaters was when she was in a school play in ninth grade. She played a drug addict. How ironic.

"You're going to be late if you don't hurry up." He leaves it at that and shuffles down the hall toward his breakfast. Craig is not bad, as far as stepdads go, I think. But I know Iris was his favorite stepdaughter. She went running with him on Saturday mornings, and he coached her soccer team from fifth grade on. Mom has never let me play sports, despite the doctors telling her repeatedly that it is perfectly safe. I watched Iris and Trista and Natalie from the sidelines, wishing I could be normal like them. But I pretend I don't care. The pale goth look works for me.

Iris never told Mom when she caught me riding Craig's motorcycle last summer. I'm still not sure if she kept quiet because she didn't want me to get in trouble, or if she was hoping I'd have a seizure and fall off. Knowing my sister, it was probably a little of both.

Two more weeks until I can try for my driver's license. I

would have taken my test on October 23, but the seizure on October 17, the Friday night before that, changed everything. That was the night my sister died and my world fell apart. I have to be seizure-free for six months before my doctor will clear me to drive. The new date is circled on the calendar over my dresser. Only fourteen days until freedom.

CHAPTER 2

We started reading *Antigone* in World Lit yesterday, and I have discovered a kindred soul. In my personal mythology, there is now Antigone, goddess of suicides and dysfunctional families. Okay, so I know she wasn't really a goddess, but she was pretty cool. And she had a father who died. And a dead sibling she missed terribly.

There were four of us. Our parents tried for years and years to have children. First came one boy, and then another, both miscarriages. Then came the fertility drugs and two twin girls, one with infantile seizures caused by hypoxia. My sister stole my oxygen before we were born. And Mom never let her forget it. She told us that the stress of my expensive NICU stay and the long nights of worrying over me as I slept in my bassinet caused Dad to sink into a deep depression. She blamed his suicide when we were two on Iris's prenatal selfishness as well.

No matter how many times I told Iris not to listen to Mom, I think deep down inside Iris believed her. She would laugh and shrug it off, but she never denied it.

It rained all day today and all day yesterday and all the day before. I'm tired of the dreariness and the damp. It's been an endless cold and wet winter. I'm actually starting to miss the sunshine.

In Advanced Algebra, I daydream. I recopy the poem "Invictus" in my notebook:

> . . . *And yet the menace of the years*
> *Finds and shall find me unafraid.*
> *It matters not how strait the gate,*
> *How charged with punishments the scroll.*
> *I am the master of my fate,*
> *I am the captain of my soul.*

I hate algebra. I hate thinking about numbers that aren't really there. I hate worrying that the teacher is going to make me write my homework on the board.

> *My head is bloodied but unbowed . . .*

I decide to share my favorite poem with the other poor souls that sit in this desk in other blocks. The teacher has her back turned, scrawling more nonsense on the chalkboard. I scribble on the desk:

> *Out of the night that covers me*
> *Black as the Pit from pole to pole*
> *I thank whatever gods may be*
> *For my unconquerable soul.*

There. Have a little goth with your binomial equations.

Lunch is a cold can of Diet Coke. I don't feel like eating. I don't feel like talking to anyone either.

The library is my favorite place at school. I usually spend my lunch period hanging out in here. The librarian grins when she sees me. "I got a new issue of *Astronomy* in," she says. "Want to see it?"

"Sure." I shrug off my backpack and sit on one of the stools behind the counter.

"I hear you might be in the market for some extra credit."

"For which class?" I ask. I am currently in danger of failing all of them. Which has everyone worried and whispering. I always was a straight-A student. Iris was too, until last spring.

"Literature, of course." Verla adjusts her glasses primly. "Someone just donated a huge collection of poetry and I don't have time to catalog and shelve all of it. I have a conference to attend this weekend and I want to have the books cataloged and ready for National Poetry Month."

I'm keeping my head above water in Mr. Herrington's class right now, but I do love poetry. I shrug noncommittally as I flip through her magazine, and soon become absorbed in an article about black widow pulsars. Before I know it, the bell rings. Reluctantly, I slide the journal back across the counter to Verla.

"You can bring it back later," she says, waving me off. "And then we'll talk about the extra credit."

Trista ambushes me as I walk to my seat in World Lit. "We're sneaking wine coolers in to see that new vampire movie."

We did that once before, with Iris. It seemed fun at the time, but I don't remember much of the movie. That was when I learned why my doctor said not to mix alcohol and seizure meds. "Not tonight. I'm not feeling good."

Trista twirls her pale blond hair around her finger as she watches me. There is a thick strand of turquoise that she's left in her hair from the weekend. So far the teachers haven't noticed. "What about this Friday? There's a keg party at some granola house near the college."

"I'll let you know." But I'm already certain I won't go with them. It takes too much effort to do anything social. They were Iris's teammates and are desperate for me to fill the Iris-shaped hole in their lives. Especially Trista.

Natalie comes in and sits behind me. She plays with my medic alert bracelet and asks me the same question she asks every day. "So?"

I smile and shake my head. "No seizures," I whisper.

She grins. "Fourteen days to go!" I think she and Tris are both as anxious for me to get my license as I am. Superbrain Natalie skipped a grade, so she won't be sixteen until August, and Tris's parents won't buy her a car. I have Iris's baby blue Volkswagen waiting for me in the garage at home. But I'd trade it in a heartbeat to have her back.

"We're going to throw the biggest party when you get your license," Trista says. "And then we're going on a road trip!" She never gives up, and I do kinda love her for that. Maybe they can accept an Andria into their group instead of an Iris.

I fiddle with my bracelet. It's a pretty custom-made one my mom bought me, with pink and purple beads, so I wouldn't have to wear a plain silver chain. But it makes me feel like I'm five. I almost wish I hadn't told Trista and Natalie about my countdown. I don't want to let them down. Iris isn't here to drive us around anymore, so the pressure is on me.

I open my Lit book.

Mr. Herrington flips his book open on the podium as well. "Let's talk about one of the major themes in *Antigone*." He writes on the chalkboard: *God's laws vs. man's laws.*

In case you haven't had to read it yet, Antigone is the daughter of Oedipus, the guy who killed his father, the king of Thebes, and married his mother, the queen. Eew. But he didn't realize it until after they'd had four kids—two sons and two daughters. When he finally figured out why the gods were cursing his kingdom with a plague, he blinded himself from shame and ran off screaming into the wilderness. His sons grew up and fought over who would rule Thebes. The one son went and got an army of Thebes's worst enemies and attacked his brother, who controlled the Theban army. The brothers killed each other, and the kingdom passed to the nearest male heir, Creon, who was Antigone's uncle. Or stepdad, according to some versions. He decreed that Eteocles, the son who died defending Thebes, would be given a hero's burial. His brother, Polyneices, who brought the enemies to the gates of Thebes, would be left in the desert to rot. This is what set Antigone off. Her brother's immortal soul was at stake here.

Natalie raises her hand. "I think Antigone placed her gods' laws above the laws of her uncle. She wanted to do what the gods wanted and give her brother a proper burial, even though Creon ordered that he be left unburied."

"Excellent. What about Creon?" Mr. Herrington asks.

"He placed his own laws first," Kimber says. "He wasn't afraid of any gods."

"He didn't want to let a girl get the better of him," Nathan says.

Several of the girls in class giggle.

The teacher rolls his eyes. "Yes, we do have some gender issues to discuss as well with these characters. But let's get back to the laws of the time. Why did Creon feel he was above the laws of the gods?"

I tune out and start doodling in my notebook. I don't turn around, but I can tell Trista and Natalie are looking at me. I've heard them whispering back and forth, and I'm certain they are worried about my mental health. About me still mourning my sister.

One thing I think I have, that my sister didn't, is hope. Or at least, a belief that things will always get better. Iris believed the worst things would always happen. I choose to ignore such possibilities, probably to the point of being stupidly naïve. I believe that bad things always happen for a reason, and that everything works out in the end. But if I ever give up on hope, then I think I will be in trouble.

CHAPTER 3

Thirteen Days

The kitchen is empty. Mom has already left for work, but has faithfully left a plate of eggs and turkey bacon and whole wheat toast in the microwave for me. My pills are sitting out on the counter, next to a glass of orange juice. Craig has already left as well. My mom and stepfather both work for one of the biggest realty firms in the county, and today he and Mom are meeting with a subdivision developer.

I pour the juice down the sink, feed the eggs and bacon to the dog, and take my pills with a Diet Coke. I am wearing a flannel plaid jumper with a long-sleeved black T-shirt and my Doc Martens. I'm going for emo Laura Ingalls today. The brisk cold snap didn't last long. The air outside is muggy and smells smoky. Someone is burning dead leaves. I take in a deep breath, trying to forget the nightmare I just had. Iris was trying to slap me, and I woke up still feeling the sting on my cheek.

In Advanced Algebra I have a surprise. Someone liked my

poetry. Or at least they liked William Ernest Henley's poetry. My lines are erased, but there are new lines scratched in tiny handwriting on the top of my desk:

> *Within my breast there is no light*
> *But the cold light of stars;*
> *I give the first watch of the night*
> *To the red planet Mars.*

That's not from "Invictus." But it sounds vaguely familiar. The teacher is passing out last week's test on imaginary numbers, so I discreetly erase the poetry off my desk. I draw a smiley face out of the 68 on my test paper. Across the top of my desk, I write,

> *Beyond this place of wrath and tears*
> *Looms but the horror of the shade.*

At lunchtime, Trista and Natalie corner me in the library. I am sitting at one of the computers, googling lines of poetry. Longfellow. That's who my mysterious desk mate was quoting. "The Light of Stars." My skin prickles, and I wonder if this mysterious algebra person loves to look at the night sky as much as I do.

> *Oh, fear not in a world like this,*
> *and thou shalt know erelong,*
> *Know how sublime a thing it is*
> *to suffer and be strong.*

I copy the lines into my notebook for later. *How sublime to suffer and be strong.* I wonder about the person who left these words on the desk. Do they suffer as much as me?

"What the hell are you reading?" Trista asks, peeking over

my shoulder at the screen. "Honey, you need to get out and have fun. You need to get laid."

"How was the movie?" I ask, sliding my notebook back into my messenger bag and closing the search engine window on the computer. I hope she ignores my blush. She knows I'm a virgin.

"Absolutely wicked. Do you want to hear what Natalie and Thomas did in the back row?"

Natalie says nothing, but gives me a wide-eyed, innocent-looking smile.

"Not now. What brought you guys in here? It must be the apocalypse if you stepped foot inside the library willingly."

Trista glances at Natalie and grins. "We're going on a mission. Should you wish to accompany us, you will be sworn to secrecy or possibly sold to Armenians."

"Oh, let's go ahead and tell her," Natalie says. "She really should come with us!"

Trista shrugs and looks back at me. "There's a new pub that opened over by the university. We're going to check out the fried mozzarella sticks. Wanna come?"

I start to say no, just as I always do. They've been trying to include me in stuff ever since Iris's death. As if they could fill the emptiness inside me with fried food and winter dances and hooking up with boys. Which makes me love them even more than I ever did before. Sometimes I feel bad, because I know they are hurting just like I'm hurting. But I can't fix myself, not yet. Not even for them.

But today, I'm willing to at least fake it. For their sakes. "Okay."

Natalie's green eyes grow huge behind her glasses. "Really?"

I shrug. "I'm not in any hurry to go home." Mom has been obsessing lately about her position on the homeowner's association. And ranting about some new neighbors that have moved in nearby. I'd rather not listen to that any more than I have to.

"Wow. You actually want to hang out with us?" Trista says. I have stunned her. But she tugs on one of my black curls. "All right, then. We can walk there from school."

Hours later, the three of us are standing outside the Indigo Dragon, a new café in Five Points, near the university. It's snuggled in between an upscale salon and an uppity children's clothing store. Outside, a carved mermaid with turquoise hair looms over the entrance. As Trista opens the front door, a waft of fresh baked bread hits us in the face. A very cute boy with close-cropped hair in a black T-shirt is leaning over the front counter, reading a magazine. I feel sick to my stomach as I recognize him.

"Oh my god, it's Pluto Alex!" Trista exclaims in obviously fake surprise. "Hi, Alex!"

He looks up and grins at Trista and Natalie. "Ladies! How's it going?"

The last time I saw Alex Hammond, he was strung out on heroin, just as high as my sister. That was the night Iris died. And I'd hoped I would never lay eyes on the bastard again.

Trista leans up against the counter. "When did you get back in town?"

No one had bothered to tell me he was back from rehab. Everyone calls him Pluto Alex because he's always been way out there. Like effing Pluto.

"Last week," Alex is saying. "I was back in class Monday. Where have you been?"

No one told me rehab made a boy grow muscles like that either. Alex was a scrawny rocker boy with scruffy long hair when he dated Iris. He still has the tattoos on his arms, but oh my god, those arms have gotten muscular.

I glare at him with all the hate my short frame can summon. If I had lasers for eyes, he'd be a puddle of goo. It's a waste of emotion, though. He's focusing on Trista.

As most boys do. Still, it's been less than six months since my sister died. You'd think Iris's boyfriend would still be mourning her.

No, I'm being a bitch. Trista is gorgeous. And even though she already has a boyfriend, she's always had a thing for broken boys. Alex is about as broken as they come.

He comes closer to me. He smells like fresh-baked bread. His smile is gone, and he looks nervous. "How have you been?"

"How do you think?" I spit out. And immediately feel bad. I stare at the menu on the board behind him. I'm thinking I'll get the fried dill pickles here, if they have good dipping sauce for them. My sister loved fried mushrooms. She would have loved this place with its quirky but oh-so-hipster vibe. "Rehab looks good on you," I admit, grudgingly.

He exhales, reaching up to scrub his newly shorn head. "Adventure therapy. The parents found a holistic center up in the mountains where I kayaked and hiked through my addiction. Been clean since that night, Andria."

And he's cleaned up pretty well. His eyes are a clear blue. An irresistible blue. I can't believe I just thought that. He was a junkie, just like my sister. And while it's freaking wonderful he was able to turn his life around, I hate that my sister didn't get the chance.

"See anything interesting?" he asks. He's too close in my personal space. I feel like I can't breathe around him. Alex Hammond, drummer of Calcifer, has always been a larger-than-life person to me. Just like Iris.

"Are the pickles good?" I ask, stepping back.

His smile is slow and wicked. "They're so good they'll make you—"

"Never mind," I say, cutting him off before he says something gross. "I'll just have the chicken Caesar salad."

He shakes his head and his lips curl into a smirk that I want to slap. "I was just going to say they'll make you order seconds." He fills out the order slip and slides it back to the kitchen. "God, Andria. Do you have a perverted mind or something?"

I glare at him and his ridiculous grin while Trista positions herself closer. "I'll take the pickles," she says. "With extra dipping sauce."

I follow Natalie and slide into the nearest booth after her. "This is a really cool place," she says, looking at the decorations on the wall. "It must be fun working here."

"My moms bought it. I'm just slave labor." Alex has followed Trista to the booth, balancing a tray of drinks, a bowl of salsa, and a basket of chips.

"Moms?" Natalie asks.

I pull the tortilla chips toward me. I know from Iris that Alex has lesbian parents, but I also know he doesn't volunteer that information freely. I guess Iris told Trista but not Natalie.

Trista slides into the seat across from us, and looks up at Alex. "Come sit with us and talk. There doesn't seem to be much of a crowd yet."

Alex stares at me, as if asking for permission. I concentrate on the salsa instead. "Thanks, but I have to get back to the counter," he says. "Got a few carryout orders to bag and I don't want you to wait too long for your food."

"PLUTO!!!" Two mop-haired guys push the front door open and walk in. A frown passes across Alex's face so swiftly I might have imagined it.

But then he grins and looks like Pluto Alex again. "Have a seat, guys. Be with you in a second."

His bandmates. Iris used to call them Thing One and Thing Two. Trista and Thing One have been on-again, off-again since last summer. Today they're off, judging by the frosty look Tris is giving him.

"Aww," Natalie says, ignoring Trista. "But yeah, we're really hungry, so go. Go get us nourishment."

Alex's gaze turns to me once more before he goes back to the counter. I'm glad if I make him uncomfortable. I hate that I'm going to have to see him in school again, but if we both put in some effort, I'm sure we can avoid each other just fine.

CHAPTER 4

Twelve Days

I answer my phone, and I know it's Iris on the other end, trying to talk to me, but I can't understand her. I beg her to speak louder, but her voice fades in and out. The only words I can hear are "don't forget." "What?" I shout. "Don't forget what?"

I open my eyes to a dark room. Once again, my nightmares haven't let me sleep more than a few hours. I glance at my clock and see my phone lying on the bedside stand, the screen lit from a recent text. A chill creeps over my damp skin. It's only a little after four. Who is texting me at this hour?

I get up and go to the bathroom for a glass of water, avoiding the phone. I know it's not really my sister, but as creepy as it sounds, I still want to entertain that possibility for just a moment longer, while I'm still half-asleep and dream-drunk.

I drink my water slowly, and hear the phone vibrate against my nightstand. With a sigh, I set the glass down and go back into the bedroom. I reach for my robe. I might as well go out and check the telescope. I slide the phone in my pocket and slip on some flip-flops.

My dog Sophie raises her head from the foot of my bed, and I bend down to scratch her behind her ears. Appeased, she goes back to sleep. I don't need her to follow me everywhere, even though she used to go to school with me when I was younger, when my meds didn't control my seizures very well. Officially, she's "retired" from being a service dog, but she still sleeps in my room and snuggles against me when I have the rare seizure.

The phone vibrates again in my pocket, and Sophie's ears prick back. I hold my breath and take it out to peek.

A text from AT&T with an offer for a new upgrade. Seriously? My heart is pounding for a spam text? "It's okay," I whisper to Sophie, and head downstairs. The house is silent except for the hum of Craig's CPAP machine in the master bedroom. I slip out onto the back deck and look up, wondering where I should point the telescope.

It's cold, but clear for once. The night sky is a perfect velvet black and the stars bright and glittering.

A dog barks down the street. Probably the terrier the Ellisons let stay outside all night. He barks at everything.

Gemini. The twins are certainly worth looking at this morning. But the house's gabled roof blocks my view. Screw it. I pick up the telescope and carry it around the side to the front yard. Mom would have kittens if she caught me out here in the dark, but it's not like there's anyone else around. I set the telescope down in the driveway and start searching for the stars Castor and Pollux.

What I see through the lens is breathtaking: Castor a bright, white double star, and Pollux, its brighter orange sibling. Off to the right of the twins, I find Betelgeuse, the pinkish-red star from Orion.

A branch from the neighbor's crêpe myrtle is blocking my

view of the nebula in Orion. Frowning, I push the telescope farther down the driveway, until I'm close to the street. It's an old neighborhood, full of historic houses, and we have far too many trees for my liking.

I take a chance and move the telescope out into the street. We live on a dead end, so I'm pretty sure no one is going to come blowing through here at four in the morning. Most of our neighbors are retired old couples anyway, who almost never leave their homes unless it's to go play golf.

I'm adjusting the focus, when I get a strange feeling. I look up and down Azalea Cove, not seeing anyone. There's no real breeze to speak of, and the subdivision is silent. Even the dog at the end of the block has grown quiet.

I'm getting chills up and down my arms. I'm scaring myself. There's no one out here, I tell myself. Everyone is inside their houses, sleeping like normal people. I consider going back inside, but I don't know when I'll have the chance to see the nebula again. There hasn't been a night this clear in weeks. I need one last look.

And then I hear the footsteps approaching. Too close. Too late to push my telescope out of the way, I stupidly stand by to defend it. And am run down by a jogger. Or possibly a serial killer.

"Son of a bitch!" I scream, just as the jogger mutters his own string of four-letter words. We tumble, tangling arms and legs and landing on the asphalt. I hear the telescope hit the ground, scraping metal and breaking glass.

"No!" I wail. My parents are going to kill me. My elbow is scraped, and my hip hurts from breaking my fall.

"What the hell?" A familiar voice demands above me. "Andria? What are you doing out here?"

Oh dear God. What is Alex Hammond doing lying on top of me?

"Get off!" I push at his chest. Of course he doesn't budge.

He laughs, and I can feel the rumble of his laughter under his rib cage. It makes my fingertips tingle.

A porch light comes on next door, and the Ellisons' terrier starts barking again down the street. Alex shifts, and I'm finally able to get out from under him. I scramble on my hands and knees on the pavement, feeling for pieces of my telescope.

"What. Are. You. Doing?" he asks. "Do your parents know you're out here?"

"Of course not," I hiss, as I find a shard of glass. Perfect. I'm shaking, and I pray he can't see it in the dark. It's probably not a good idea to admit I'm out here all by myself. "What are you doing out here? Waiting for your dealer?"

I hear him let out a breath and stand up. "Couldn't sleep."

"Me either," I finally say, feeling like a bitch again. He brings out the worst in me.

Alex picks up my telescope and follows me up the driveway to the front porch. "Been having nightmares ever since I came home."

I look up at him, now that I'm able to see his face. The neighbor's floodlight is pointed straight at us. He looks tired. "Nightmares about what?" I ask.

Before he can answer, the neighbors' front door opens. Alex pulls me back against the far side of our porch, where we're partially hidden by the shadows of Mom's hanging ferns. Part of me wants to get away from him, to yell for help and run back into the light, where the neighbors can see. The other part doesn't want to move.

"Are you bleeding?" he whispers, his mouth close to my ear. It sends shivers all the way down my neck.

"Shh," I whisper back. I guess I've made my decision. I'd rather stay hidden in the shadows with the addict than risk a scolding from one of the neighbors.

We're both silent, me with my hand throbbing in pain and

my heart pounding from standing so close to this boy. His skin is damp with sweat, and I try to put a little distance between us. Unfortunately, he grabs my hand so he can look at it.

I can't see from where we are who has come outside next door. Mrs. Dawes is partially deaf and legally blind, but her husband is the eyes and ears of the neighborhood. He was the one who told Mom that Iris was doing drugs. If only she'd bothered to listen to him.

I hold my breath and pray that Alex will keep his mouth shut.

It seems like forever until we hear an elderly man's cough, and his front door opens and closes again.

I let my breath out and pull my hand away from Alex.

"Did you get glass in there?" he asks.

My palm stings when I move my fingers. "I think so. I'll clean it off inside. Are you hurt?"

"Just banged up a little. Sorry I tripped over you." He steps back, thankfully. Finally, he's out of my bubble. "Why in the hell were you in the road?"

"Too many trees," I say. I shiver, now that his warmth is gone.

"We can blame all of this on the trees, then," he says, trying to make a joke. But I don't smile. He notices. "Will your parents get mad about the telescope?"

I shrug. If I can't fix it myself, then I won't be able to see the meteor shower in two weeks. "They probably won't even notice," I say. But that's the main reason I'm anxious to get my license. I want to be able to drive out to the fields south of the university and watch the Lyrids.

"I'm sorry."

I wish he'd stop saying that. "Look, I'd better get inside. My mom will be waking up soon. I'll see you around."

He rubs his hand over his head. I wonder if it's because he's still not used to the short cut. It makes him look so much different. He no longer looks like a triplet of Thing One and Thing Two. "Take care of that hand," he says.

He takes off from the porch, finishing his run. I watch him disappear into the darkness and suddenly wonder what he was doing in my neighborhood in the middle of the night. He and his moms live south of the university, according to Iris. And he never did tell me what his nightmares were about.

CHAPTER 5

Mom left whole wheat French toast and hard-boiled eggs for me this morning. I give both to Sophie. She hasn't been eating her regular food much lately, but I think it's just because she's getting old. I hope my mom's breakfasts are nutritious enough for an elderly Siberian husky. She seems to like them, and I love seeing her tail wag when I bring her breakfast on Mom's good china.

Craig catches me coming out of my bedroom with the plate, but he only smiles and shakes his head. "So that's how you keep your girlish figure," he says.

I roll my eyes and take the dish back to the kitchen.

My stepfather follows me. "What did you do to your hand?" He picks it up and turns it over, palm up, so he can look at the bandage. Before Iris died, he was never very touchy or affectionate with me. Now it seems every day he finds a reason to hug me.

"Splinter," I say, pulling my hand back. "Have to run or I'll be late for the bus."

"I can take you. I don't mind."

It's been a pain in the butt taking the bus while Iris's car waits in the garage for me. So the rare mornings he or Mom are here to drive me, I leap at the chance.

Riding to school in Craig's convertible Mercedes is painfully awkward. The vehicle is quiet, but Craig taps his hands on the steering wheel and hums along to nineties boy band music from his Pandora station. Savage Garden, I think. Or maybe Backstreet Boys.

As he pulls into the drop-off circle, he reaches over and squeezes my wrist gently. "Take care, Andria."

I don't answer, but grab my bag and hop out of the vehicle, more creeped out by his music choices than his touchy-feely-ness. I know he and Mom both think I'm frail and now that I've lost my twin I just might be fragile enough to break. As if we were attached like Siamese twins and dependent upon one another. In some ways, we were. But in other ways, we were very separate entities. Sometimes, I feel like I never really knew my sister at all. And now that she's gone, I won't ever get the chance.

★ ★ ★

There, in a black-blue vault she sails along,
Followed by multitudes of stars . . . small
And sharp, and bright, along the dark abyss

There's more poetry on the desk today. I touch the words with my fingers, as if they were braille. Mrs. Davis rambles on at the front of the class about additive inverses. I copy the poem into my notebook, wishing I had something just as beautiful to leave on the desk for my verse-loving friend.

I don't have time at lunch to look up the poem, though. I have a unit exam in chemistry tomorrow, so I sit in the courtyard with Trista, cramming. Only she's more interested in glaring at Thing One, otherwise known as Hank. Her man is flirting on the other side of the courtyard with two sophomores who are wearing Calcifer T-shirts. He has an arm draped around each giggling girl. Alex is sitting at the picnic table beside them, his head down as if he's taking a nap.

"Hey." I tap Tris's book with my pen. "Back to Boyle's law."

She flips her book closed. "I'm too pissed to study. That asshole texted me last night and said he missed me."

"Maybe he was drunk?" I ask. "Or high? You don't need a loser like him. Find someone who deserves you. Someone who's sober."

She looks at me like I've sprouted two heads. "God, Andria. Not everyone who parties is a drug addict."

Natalie gasps as she comes up and sits down beside us. "Tris!" she says, horrified.

Trista stares at her shoes. "Whatever, I know that sounds bitchy, but seriously. We don't have to stop having fun because Iris couldn't handle it."

I slam my chemistry book shut. I want to ask her if she thought Iris smoked heroin for fun, but Tris won't understand. She thinks popping pills and drinking on the weekends is innocent fun. She likes to party, but she's never done hard stuff. Nor has Natalie. At least I don't think they have.

Both of them are on the girls' soccer team. They should be more interested in keeping their bodies healthy, but I don't bother to point that out.

I still don't want to talk about Iris with anyone. And I really don't think they want to talk about her either. For months, the school looked like a funeral home, with flower wreaths and flower crosses and teddy bears and cards heaped in a growing pile in the front hall. We had counselors come and talk to us. Iris's teachers and coaches mourned along with us. I had to share my grief with the entire school. And I resented that. And now everyone else besides our dysfunctional group has moved on, and I am left alone to mourn. But I wish I could move on too.

I'm beginning to think my sister's perfect life was not so perfect, for her to abandon herself to drugs like that. Why didn't I see that sooner? I should have noticed something, should have tried to help her. I was so jealous of her social life and her love life. I'm a terrible twin for not knowing something was wrong until it was too late. And I don't want my friends to realize what a horrible person I am. I'd rather they just think I'm still mad with grief.

Before I can grab my stuff and storm off dramatically, Tris beats me to it, saving me the embarrassment. She takes her books and stomps off. She passes dangerously close to Thing One and his groupies, and it looks like she says something to him, because he drops his arms from around the girls. Alex sleeps through the drama, until Trista sits down on the table with him and rubs up against him. Thing One looks murderous, then he takes both sophomores and leaves the courtyard, his hand squeezing one's ass.

Natalie is watching the show with me. "Maybe Hank isn't the one for Tris. But they've got a lot of history, and I don't think either of them really wants to let the other one go yet. She's wasting her time with Pluto, though. He is definitely still mourning Iris."

"What makes you say that?" I ask. He is trying to ignore Tris, but she now has her hands all over him. Playing with his hair, touching his shirt. I want to smile when he tries to scoot away from her and she finally slinks off.

"I've seen him wear her ring," Natalie says.

"The opal one?" We had matching birthstone rings our parents gave us on our fifteenth birthday. Mine is still in my jewelry box. They say it's bad luck to wear opal if you weren't born in October, so I refuse to wear mine. Iris loved hers and didn't care about superstitions.

Natalie shakes her head. "Maybe? But I don't think it's opal. It looks like a galaxy or something."

I stare at her. That is my ring. The one with a stone that looks like the Butterfly Nebula. Iris gave it to me the Christmas we were freshmen, then borrowed it all the time. I haven't seen it in over a year.

"Besides," Natalie says, still watching Alex. "He's been so different since Iris died. Much more quiet than he used to be. It's like he's gone . . . dark."

"Broody dark or homicidal dark?" I ask.

She shrugs.

The bell rings, and I have to go to class. It would be rude of me to demand my ring back from Alex if it reminds him of Iris, but it's mine. Sooner or later, I'll want it back.

Natalie follows me in to English, but Tris skips. Maybe she's getting back together with Thing One and they are making out in the parking lot. I can't help but feel a tiny bit jealous, because the teacher makes us clear our desks as soon as the bell rings and hands out an exam on the previous unit, Greek comedies and Aristophanes.

Answer four of the following five essay questions. Each question is worth twenty-five points. I just spent the last thirty minutes studying the wrong thing.

CHAPTER 6

Eleven Days

A 47. I flunked yesterday's test on Greek comedies utterly. Tragically. I wonder if Verla is some sort of psychic. Not only did I miss lunch today because I had to help Natalie study for French, but my bracelet broke and I thought I had lost it. Luckily, Natalie found it in the grass in the quad. I don't know if the clasp can be replaced or not.

After going over the exam, our teacher wants to continue discussing themes in Antigone. And Mr. Herrington wants to talk about Antigone's relationship with her sister, Ismene. I slump a little in my seat, and avoid Natalie's gaze. Antigone was the outspoken one, and Ismene was the one who wanted to follow the rules. No, she wanted to follow their uncle's rules. Antigone wanted to follow the rules of their gods. Ismene tried to play it safe, but then also tried to stand up for her sister when Antigone was arrested. "Kill me too," Ismene begged, when Antigone got the death penalty, which only pissed Antigone off. In a sense, Iris and I are like Ismene and Antigone.

I am the freak with the strange disease who doesn't want to dress like anyone else. My sister wasn't quiet, but she definitely tried to fit in with everyone. But Ismene didn't die. Antigone is the one who dies, by committing suicide before Creon can kill her. She chooses to face death on her own terms.

What a way to get behind your principles. Ismene might be scorned by her sister for being too weak to stand up for what she believes in, but she knows her family has suffered enough and pleads with Antigone to make peace with their uncle. But as a result of Antigone being stubborn and standing up for what she believes in, she dies, her boyfriend dies, and his mom dies. A high price to pay for one's beliefs. Or is that being too proud to back down?

Yes, Creon suffers too. His son and wife both commit suicide. He goes mad with grief.

There is no happy ending in this story. Ismene is left completely alone, knowing her sister died without forgiving her. She's lost the last members of her family by the end of the play.

Our teacher points out the difference between the various suicides in Antigone. The main character kills herself because she's accepted her fate, and is willing to die for her beliefs. Haemon and his mother kill themselves because they are unhappy with their fates, unwilling to live without their loved ones.

Natalie is scribbling something furiously on a sheet of notebook paper. Trista is staring out the window, looking bored. The rest of the girls from the soccer team are tearing up dramatically, wiping mascara from their cheeks.

I roll my eyes so that they don't water. I can't cry in here. I did not cry when Iris died and I won't cry now with the rest of these drama queens. Iris's death was officially deemed an accident. Not a suicide. But don't you have to have some sort of death wish to smoke heroin?

Natalie's note lands on my desk. "Do you need to go to the nurse? I can take you if, you know, you might suddenly feel weak or dizzy. We could just go to the bathroom instead. Or we could go to Disney World. I'm here for you. Mr. Herrington is an obtuse dick."

I have to laugh. Which makes everyone look at me. The ones who think I'm about to commit suicide because I'm so depressed about my twin sister's death. The ones who have been whispering all along that her overdose was intentional. The ones who call me Abby instead of Andria because they think I look like the goth chick on *NCIS*. (And I really don't— Iris used to call my style more grunge than goth.)

I don't even own any black leather besides my boots. My hair is naturally black and curly, thanks to our Greek grandparents, even though Iris was only half as lucky. She always envied my curls while I lusted after her sleek raven locks.

I laugh because Natalie is going into battle mode. Planning our retreat before the opposition attacks. Scorch and burn. I raise my hand. Natalie's eyes widen as she prepares to get up with me. But I'm standing my ground. "Mr. Herrington? Do you think Ismene's end is more tragic or Antigone's? Because if Antigone had listened to Ismene, they'd both still be alive. Haemon and his mom would still be alive, too."

"It depends on the reader," our teacher says. "Do you feel your beliefs are worth dying for?"

I have no beliefs. But I don't say that. Perhaps I am more like Ismene, unwilling to speak out for fear of upsetting the status quo.

Mr. Herrington continues, apparently not expecting an answer from me. "You might agree with Ismene, and think the ends justifies the means. That moral integrity is not worth the sacrifice of even one human life. But the ancient Greeks thought

Antigone was right. That by standing up for her beliefs, she died an honorable death."

All this time, I've been pretty sure my sister didn't choose to die. Not that we'll ever know for sure, but what fate would she have been trying to avoid? She had it pretty good until the drugs got out of control. She had an adoring group of friends, a hot boyfriend, a driver's license, and a wicked car our parents bought for her. Decent grades and a few trophies for playing soccer on a championship team. She was healthy. Normal.

But now I wonder. What did she believe? Did she believe her life was hopeless? Did she think drugs were a way to escape something she didn't think she could handle anymore? If so, Iris, why couldn't I have changed your mind?

There is no happy ending in this story, I write across the top of my Antigone notes.

Exhausted and hungry and depressed, I drag my butt into the library after class to beg and plead for Verla's extra-credit assignment. I don't think it will be any problem sorting through old books of poetry. If I don't bring my English grade up to a C or better, my parents won't let me take the driving test, seizure-free or not.

Someone else is talking to Verla in the tiny office behind her desk. I hop up onto the desk to wait, looking at one of the books she has lying there.

Robert Frost. I'm flipping through the pages, reading about fire and ice and snow and stars, when they come out of the office.

"Oh, Andria," Verla is saying. "I'm glad you're here too. This will be your extra-credit partner."

I don't have to look up to know who it is. My luck sucks that way.

Alex Hammond drops his book bag on the floor and steals the book from my hands.

Of course it's him.

I glare at Verla. "I haven't agreed to anything yet. Do I have to work with him?"

She looks from one of us to the other, startled. I see in her eyes the moment she realizes what she's done. She's heard the whispers and the rumors. This is the boy who killed my sister. She takes the stack of books in her arms and cradles them close to her chest. "I don't see how we can do this any other way. We've got to get these books cataloged by the end of next week. I'll need both of you here after school every day from three thirty to six."

Alex glances up from the book at me, but says nothing. He's daring me to chicken out. I glare right back. "How much extra credit are we talking about?"

Verla leans against the counter. "Your teacher has promised two 100s that count as test grades."

That would definitely help erase the 47. "No problem, Miss V," I say.

She breathes a visible sigh of relief. "Great. If you can make arrangements to start this afternoon, that would be wonderful."

"I'd have to call," I say. I'll need a ride home, but I'll be damned if I mention that in front of Alex.

"I'm good." Alex holds on to the Robert Frost book and follows Verla to a computer station and a stack of plastic containers filled with the donated poetry collection.

I send a message to my mom and tuck my phone back in my purse. I'm already dreading the ride home. I'll have to listen to her lecture me about my English grades.

By the time I catch up with Alex and Verla, she's showing him the catalog system on the computer. "Each book will need to be entered into the system," she's saying. "Title, author, publisher, pub date, ISBN number." She's pointing to a long line of numbers in one of the front pages of the book in her hand.

Alex moves over so I can see better.

"Once you have the book in the database, you can print out the barcode sticker and attach it to the corner of the front cover." She glances up at the tiny label printer and frowns. "I seem to be missing a cable. Well, you can still type in the information while I hunt one down. Once you're done with these crates, there are three more stacks in the back."

"Holy crap," I say. "How many books are there?"

She grins. This must seem like Christmas to her. "Five hundred volumes. Isn't this wonderful? When you're done with each one, stack it in one of the piles on this table over here. I need them alphabetized by poet names. One stack for each letter."

I nod, pulling three books out of the first crate. Anne Sexton, Sylvia Plath, Marianne Moore. "Who donated all of these books anyway?"

"The relatives of an elderly gentleman who recently passed. He'd been a professor at Vanderbilt."

Alex picks up a few more books, some that are leather bound. "And he wanted to leave his collection to a bunch of high school kids?" He shakes his head in wonder.

Verla shrugs and hurries off to find a printer cable.

Alex is right. Some of these volumes look old, even if they have been well cared for. I don't know how long they'll stay in good condition once they start getting checked out. If anyone checks them out. Not too many kids in my school can appreciate Marianne Moore.

I take my three lady poets and claim the computer closest to the window.

Alex sits at the other one, yawning. He looks as tired as I feel. I can't remember the last time I had a dream-free night. I open the first book on my pile and start typing.

We work silently alongside each other for several minutes. I don't want to talk to him, and yet I want him to say something.

No, I really don't. He'll say something about Iris, and it will make me mad.

Verla comes back and plugs in the printer. "All ready to go," she says, before disappearing again into her office.

I print a bar code for Anne Sexton's collected works, and carefully place it on the front cover. Alex still hasn't said anything. Maybe I should say something.

And then my stomach growls. And growls. My cheeks burn. Next to me, Alex snorts.

"Shut up." I pick up the next book and start typing in the information.

"I didn't see you at lunch," he says. "What was more important than a nutritious salad in a plastic box?"

I stare at him. "How do you know what I eat for lunch? Are you stalking me?"

He rolls his eyes. "Andria, you always eat salad for lunch. When you do eat. But you are obviously starving right now."

"I'm fine. We'll be going home in an hour or so." My stomach growls again in protest. Dammit.

"Six o'clock is a long time from now," he says and gets up. He disappears into Verla's office for several minutes. I ignore my stomach and concentrate on processing the books. Maybe this won't take as long as Verla thinks it will. Maybe I can volunteer to stay later than six and get it done in one or two days.

Alex sits back down and plops a bag of miniature candy bars on the desk between us. "Found her stash."

"You can't steal her candy!"

He unwraps one and pops it in his mouth. "Mmm."

"You are going to hell, Hammond."

His eyes look haunted even as he grins at me. I should not

have said that. The pain in his eyes makes something flicker in my chest. Something that has no business flickering.

"Oh, probably," he whispers. "But not for this." And then he stuffs another chocolate kiss in his mouth.

I glance down at the time on the bottom of my screen and groan. 4:05. Two more hours of torture.

CHAPTER 7

I try to ignore the chocolate and concentrate on the books, but now my head hurts from being so hungry. I begin to worry that low blood sugar might trigger a seizure. And I can't let that happen. Not in front of Alex.

4:07. With a defeated sigh, I snatch one of the chocolates from the bag.

"Welcome to the Dark Side."

"Shut up," I say, my mouth full of chocolate and caramel. Mmm. Sugar. I grab another and promise myself that's all I need to make it through the afternoon.

But I'm only lying to myself. I eat three more pieces of candy over the next two hours. Alex does not speak to me anymore, but stops working on the books every now and then to write something in his notebook. I am too busy ignoring him to ask what he's doing. I am really not interested.

By the time Verla returns, we have made it through the first two crates of books. I stand up and rub my neck, trying not to yawn.

"I'm impressed," our librarian says, peeking into the third crate. "This might not take too long after all. You'll still get the full extra credit, though." She goes to the piles of finished books on the table. "Ah, William Stafford. One of my favorites." She smooths the cover gently, as if caressing a child's face. "I can't wait to share all of these wonderful poems with you kids."

"You gotta love her for her enthusiasm," Alex says as we're walking out the front door.

I can't hear any sarcasm in his voice. I think he likes Verla as much as I do. But I shrug and pull out my phone. Mom is not here yet.

One of Alex's moms is here, though. He opens the door to her truck and looks back at me. "Need a ride?"

"My mother's coming. Besides, I thought you lived on the other side of town."

He grins as he shakes his head. "We bought the big house on Laurel Street. The one behind yours. We're neighbors."

"Oh." I can't think of anything else to say. I guess that explains his jogging the other night.

His mom leans across the front of the truck to see me. "Honey? Are you sure we can't give you a ride home?"

"No, but thank you. There's my mother now." I see her silver Lexus waiting to turn into the circle. Thank God.

Alex follows my gaze, and his eyes grow sad. I don't think he wants to see my mother right now. He looks back at me. "See you tomorrow," he says, and climbs into the truck.

Why would his moms buy the house right behind ours? I know it's on the historical register, but don't they care that his dead girlfriend's family lives nearby? They were respectful and did not attend Iris's funeral, but sent a giant peace lily. Even though I'd heard from Trista that Alex's moms thought Iris had been the bad influence on him and not the other way around.

My parents never offered to meet them once during Alex

and Iris's four months of dating. But if Mom finds out the Hammonds have moved into the neighborhood, she'll be torn between shunning them and baking them a casserole.

As soon as my mother pulls up, I climb into the car, dumping my backpack on the floor in front of me.

"That bag looks heavy," Mom says. "Do I need to speak with the school nurse about the load you're carrying around?"

"It's fine." I hate when she riles up the school nurse with petty stuff. "What's for supper?"

"I'd rather talk about your grades and why you have to stay after school every day for the next week."

I slump down in my seat. Just a little, not enough to make her comment about my posture too. "I forgot to study."

"In English? I know it's not your favorite subject, but you know you still have to pay attention to your GPA. I left a spinach and zucchini lasagna warming in the oven for you. Your father and I are having dinner with the bank's mortgage officer."

"What restaurant?"

"NONA."

"Bring me some shrimp pasta?" I ask. I can't believe they're going to my favorite restaurant without me. Even if it is for a business dinner.

"But I made you lasagna—"

"Please? And some crab cakes?" The stolen chocolates I had in the library won't hold me over for very long, but I can eat some of the lasagna, put the rest in the freezer, and wait for Mom and Craig to get home with my takeout. Even if the crab cakes are cold when she brings them to me.

She sighs as she puts her blinker on, and waits for a mini-van to pass so she can turn into our dead-end street. "No crab cakes. But I'll bring you the pasta. Only if you promise to write that essay for Duke."

She still wants me to go somewhere more prestigious than UGA. Somewhere relatively close, though, like Vanderbilt or

Duke. And she knows with the grades I used to get, I'd have no problem getting accepted. But not with the grades I'm making now. She's afraid of my going too far away for school. Because whatever would I do halfway across the country if I had a seizure?

The same thing I do when I have a seizure here. Pick myself up and carry on. At least halfway across the country, I wouldn't have to worry about hurting people I love.

CHAPTER 8

Ten Days

Iris is standing at the foot of my bed, her eyes dark with fury. But she won't say anything, and I'm frightened by her chilly stare. She wants me to apologize, to make things right, but I can't. With a soundless cry, she reaches for me, grabs my arms.

I sit up in bed, my heart pounding. My hair clings to my damp neck. Another effing nightmare. I rub my arm to find a long scratch, the skin around it turning an angry red. I must have done it to myself in my sleep. I keep my eyes open, to make sure the vision of my sister doesn't return. Not like that. I don't like the Iris of my dreams.

I grab my robe and sneak downstairs to make a cup of strong coffee. There is no way I'm going back to sleep now. The clock on the microwave says 4:45. It should be getting light soon. Too late now to do any stargazing. Not that I have a working telescope anyway.

It was late when Mom and Craig got home last night, but

I stayed up and wrote my essay and waited for them, holding out for my favorite food. This is what I get every year for my birthday dinner. Mom was true to her word, and I got to go to bed with a happy tummy, even if it was close to midnight.

I stare out the window across the backyard, wondering if my mother knows that Alex and his parents moved in behind us. I wouldn't be surprised. She is the president of the neighborhood historical society and vice president of the gardening club. And as a real estate agent, she knows the financial details of every property in Clarke County. She probably knows exactly how old the Hammond house's water heater is and exactly how many square feet their garage is. Not terribly juicy information, but she's been Agent of the Year at her office almost every year since I can remember. It must mean something to somebody.

At least the Hammonds haven't turned on the floodlights. Our backyard is one huge moonshadow, shaded by the pine trees and the holly bushes that separate our property from theirs. I wonder if Alex is still having nightmares too.

No, I really don't care about him or his nightmares. I have my own demons to deal with. I try to be quiet as I start the coffeemaker, but Sophie waddles into the kitchen, her happy tail thumping against the wall as she comes down the hallway. She wants to go outside and bark at squirrels. But that would piss off our neighbors this early in the morning, so I shush her with an oatmeal cookie from the cookie jar.

Mom made the cookies last weekend, with a gluten-free recipe she found online. Quinoa Oatmeal Cranberry Cookies. They're actually not bad. And Sophie loves them. With a mother who's a five-time winner of the Best Shade Garden award for Pine Hills and who bakes homemade healthy treats for her children, you'd think we'd have the perfect family. But of course, you would be horribly wrong.

My mother comes into the kitchen and catches me dumping an extra-large spoonful of sugar in my coffee. "What on earth arc you doing?" she exclaims, horrified. "You shouldn't even be drinking coffee!"

I try not to roll my eyes. "Doctor Ly says it's fine in moderation."

She takes the mug away from me with a hurt glare and pours it down the sink. "You're too young to be starting bad habits. Let me fix you a proper breakfast. With a glass of orange juice."

My fingernails dig into my palms, but I can't keep from smarting off. "No, you wouldn't want me to succumb to bad habits, would you? It starts with coffee, but before long I'd need something harder and next thing you know, I'd be hooked on Red Bull. And then, I'd turn to . . ." I see her eyes widen, but I can't stop my mouth from moving. Can't stop myself from saying words that I know will hurt. "Meth."

Mom drops the mug. It makes a loud noise but thankfully doesn't shatter. Sophie whines at us, visibly upset by the tension in the kitchen.

I'm shocked at myself. And at Mom, for actually showing emotion. But as soon as I start to feel guilty, she blinks and picks up the mug. "It's obvious you've already had too much sugar. It always does make you overly emotional."

I bite my tongue in a superhuman effort not to say anything overly emotional. Instead, I open the door to let Sophie outside. She takes off across the yard as a squirrel scampers to safety up the nearest oak tree. Go ahead, Soph. Bark all you want at those pesky squirrels. Mr. Dawes is probably awake already and desperate for neighborhood gossip anyway.

Mom goes to the freezer and pulls out a box of whole grain waffles. "How about these? And a soft-boiled egg?"

"They taste like thawed-out cardboard. Mom, please. I don't need you to keep making me breakfast every morning. I'll be fine. I can eat a cereal bar or a piece of toast."

She tosses the waffles back in the freezer with a huff. "I know you can fix yourself something. But breakfast is the one thing I know how to do. Because obviously I don't know how to be a good mother."

I reach out for her without another thought and hold her in my arms, feeling like a terrible daughter. She's shaking, and I know she hates confrontation just as much as me. She sniffs, and I feel sick. Why did I have to set her off?

Of course she's a good mother. Hasn't she always taken care of me and protected me? Made sure I went to my doctor appointments and took my medicine? It's not like she beat Iris or willfully neglected her. Iris and I always had the same allowance, the same curfew. As long as we were together, we were treated equally as a pair. Mom made more of a fuss over me, but she still loved Iris.

I want to tell her not to be too hard on herself. That Iris's death wasn't her fault. But before I can say anything, she pulls away and retreats down the hallway back to her bedroom. I'm left alone in the kitchen, though I'm too upset now to eat anything.

But I still need caffeine. No matter what my mother says. I leave for school early in order to take the scenic route and hike to Jittery Joe's. I can catch my school bus a block past the coffeehouse if I time it right. I grab my too-heavy book bag and leave the house without saying anything else to Mom. Without upsetting her any more than I already have.

It's chilly this morning, and I start to regret my stubborn need for a stimulant-laden mocha. I wore the thickest, coziest socks that I could squeeze into my black boots, but my toes are almost numb by the time I reach Joe's. My favorite barista, Maddy, winks at me and makes my usual: a skinny mocha with extra whipped cream and a chocolate drizzle. I warm myself with the drink, but it hits my stomach like acid. I hate fighting with Mom. I should have just let her make the waffles for me. It would have made her happy. And I'd be able to feel my feet right now.

Natalie is waiting at the bus stop when I get there. She smiles when I share my mocha with her. Maddy has drawn a cute bunny vampire next to my name on the cup today. A Bunnicula for Easter. "Very cute," Natalie says, admiring the artwork. "Mmm, and very yummy. Today is Day Ten, yes?"

I automatically reach for my bracelet, forgetting it's still broken and sitting on my dresser. My stomach knots up even more. I want my license more than anything, but I'm so scared something bad will happen before I get to take the test.

"Where do you want to go to celebrate when you pass?" she asks as she hands the cup back to me.

No one knows about the meteor shower. That will be a secret trip. Iris loved stargazing too when we were little, but I don't feel like sharing my night sky with anyone else. "I don't know," I say. "Probably to the mall? We could eat at the Mexican place."

But Natalie has taken it upon herself to plan a Major Outing for this life event. She is discussing our options in first block with Trista, who favors a day trip to Atlanta.

"Um, no." The thought of driving in that traffic terrifies me.

"Ooh, Six Flags!" Natalie says.

"Please no," I say. I sketch tiny stars inside the cover of my notebook. Swirly spiral Van Gogh stars.

Tris frowns. "Iris would have loved Six Flags. I think we should go in her honor."

I am not Iris. And I don't think I'll ever replace her in Trista's eyes. They were best friends since seventh grade, and Natalie and I became best friends sort of by default. With Iris gone, our circle is out of balance. I feel bad for Trista, and sometimes I think she misses Iris just as much as I do. Only she has a different way of mourning. Just when I think she's healing, she says something like this and my own wounds reopen.

Our chemistry teacher begins calling attendance, and Natalie gives me one last sad glance before turning around in her seat. I roll my eyes at Trista. And yet I worry that I will give in and take them to Atlanta in the end. Just to keep the peace. But I'm scared that if I start giving in to Trista's wishes now, what if I don't stop until I've become her substitute Iris? I might just start wearing bright colors and playing soccer. Dating broody rocker boys.

Never. Going. To. Happen.

But what if it did, and what if I actually prefer my sister's life to my own?

CHAPTER 9

In French, Natalie keeps throwing out suggestions. The river. The mall. The zoo. I am getting a headache.

She sighs and pats me on the shoulder. "Don't worry. We won't make you drive to Six Flags. This is for you. And I don't think Iris would have made you go somewhere just because she liked it either. Trista will get over it."

I'm thankful that Natalie hasn't changed through all of this. She is still my shy best friend, sad that we've lost Iris, but patient with me and Tris both in our depression. Natalie is still our mother hen, as well as the best defense player our girls' soccer team has ever had. And if she's gotten closer to Trista over the past few months, that's probably because I've pulled away from her.

By the time I get to third block, I put my head down on my binder. I'm grateful that I don't know anyone in this class. No one bothers me in here. I never thought I'd be grateful for the blissful droning of my algebra teacher. Just before I drift off, I notice new lines scribbled across the top of my desk:

This is thy hour O Soul, thy free flight into the wordless . . .
Pondering the themes thou lovest best,
Night, sleep, death and the stars.

A chill flutters over my skin. Walt Whitman. I saw that poem in the book Alex was cataloging yesterday. Oh God. Please don't let him be the desk poet. I wanted it to be someone mysterious and dark and moody. Anybody but mysterious and dark and moody Alex Hammond.

I erase the words. We both ponder the same dark themes, apparently. I can't help but shiver. It would be so easy to be friends with Alex. In theory, at least. But it would also be wrong. He dated my sister. Was a Bad Influence on my sister. Probably copying the moody poetry as his own way of mourning. I decide not to write anything back. This needs to stop.

Even though I found a poem yesterday by Longfellow that would be perfect.

I try to pay attention as the teacher drones on about polynomials. I think about Alex jogging in the middle of the night because he can't sleep. I think about how close we were standing on my porch that night, hiding from the neighbor.

And then I try to remember him stoned as Iris picked him up from band practice with Thing One and Thing Two, how he let her steal joints from his pocket. He might not have forced her to do drugs with him, he might not have shot up her arm with heroin, but yes, he was definitely a Bad Influence.

I know Iris was crazy about him, and that they dated for several months, but she never confided to me how serious they were. I never asked. I never cared.

I wonder if he ever told her he loved her. I wonder if he's haunted now with regret.

Oh, what the hell.

O holy Night! from thee I learn to bear
What man has borne before!
Thou layest thy finger on the lips of Care
And they complain no more.

I'm nervous about going to the library today. I don't know if I should ask Alex about the desk poems or if I should keep it a secret that I know. Maybe it's not him after all. Or maybe he's known it's me he's writing to all along. What if it's just a game to him? What is he getting out of it?

That afternoon we sit side by side in the library, silently skimming through the stacks of poetry. I start to have my doubts. He occasionally writes something down in his notebook, but would he do that right in front of me if he knew I knew about the desk in math?

"Who is your favorite poet?" I finally ask.

Alex turns his body toward me, as if he's been waiting all along for me to say something first, to let him know it's okay to talk to me. "It changes from week to week," he says. "This week I like Walt Whitman. Who is yours?"

Oh God, it really is him. "It changes for me too," I say, and look back at my computer screen. If I told him Longfellow, would he get the hint? I don't know which block he takes his math in, so he might not have seen my desk poem yet. And I am reluctant to tell him the truth. He might decide to quit writing. I can't help but look forward to seeing his handwriting on my desk every day. "My all-time favorite is Sylvia Plath," I say finally.

He nods. "Good stuff. *Ariel,* 'Lady Lazarus.'"

I frown. He would like the depressing ones. "'The Moon and the Yew Tree'?"

He rubs his hair again self-consciously. "I started reading poems out loud to myself because I like to hear the rhythm

DREAMING OF ANTIGONE 51

and the sound of the words. To me that's just as important as the meaning of the words. Plath's way with word crafting is magical."

I get this. He's a songwriter. Of course these things are important to him. I want to ask him if he also likes to commit random acts of graffiti with his favorite poems. But I can't. I want to keep his secret to myself just a little while longer. What if there's someone else who sits at our desk, someone else he's writing to? I shouldn't mind, but for some stupid reason, the thought bothers me. "I think the older poems have more of a rhythm. They're more song-like."

"Are you going to the party at Lucy's this weekend?" he asks. Now that he feels it's safe to talk to me, it's like he doesn't want to stop. "Calcifer is going to play."

The band drifted in limbo for the three months he's been in rehab. Thing One and Thing Two didn't bother looking for another singer. They were content to spend their weekends playing the Xbox and getting baked. Alex apparently has the band back in business. Well, good for him.

"Not really into the senior parties," I say. "But congratulations on going back to your old life."

His eyes lose their sparkle, and I feel like a bitch. I didn't mean for it to come out sounding so bitter. Well, maybe I did, but I didn't mean for it to hurt him so badly.

"It's not the same," he whispers. "I don't want to go back to my old life. I want—"

But before Alex can tell me what he wants, the double doors to the library bang open and Verla pushes another extra-large plastic tote full of books inside. She slides the tote across the room to where we are. I swear a cloud of dust rises up from inside it.

"Look! The family found another closet they hadn't gone through," she says. "Could be another fifty or sixty books in here."

Which means at least one more day of cataloging and data entering. I don't know if I can still do this without strangling Alex. Or without him wanting to strangle me.

He stands and grabs the tote from her, lifting it easily onto the table. "Ooh, more brooding Victorians," he says, peering inside. His eyes light up as he pulls out a book and hands it to me.

Christina Rossetti. I shake my head with a tiny smile, ignoring the way my stomach flutters.

Paging through, I find the words I will write on the desk in algebra tomorrow.

I never watch the scatter'd fire
Of stars, or sun's far-trailing train,
But all my heart is one desire,
And all in vain

CHAPTER 10

Nine Days

I awake to my alarm and Sophie's tail wagging violently against my dresser, which is a surprise. A whole night's sleep without any nightmares. I'm suspicious, but definitely grateful. Even if I don't feel particularly rested. I might not have dreamed of Iris, but I tossed and turned for hours worrying about her. Why I never knew she was taking drugs. Why I never knew how unhappy she was. Even if she didn't die on purpose, something made her unable to cope and made her think drugs were the only way to escape. Something was making her miserable. And she felt trapped.

What could I have done differently? I should have known. I should have been there for her.

My cell phone lights up and vibrates on my bedside stand. It is six thirty in the morning. And there are two words on my phone's screen when I pick it up.

Help me.

I tear myself out of bed, leaving my phone in the folds of

the sheets. My heart pounds, and I feel a tingly dizziness in my head from jumping up so fast.

The snooze tone goes off again, and I have to pick it up before it wakes anyone else up. My fingers are shaking as I reach for the phone. *Dammit, just do it, Andria.*

And the screen is blank when I finally screw up my courage to peek at it again. I press the "Home" button, to make my phone light back up, but the text message is gone.

It was just a nightmare. Or am I starting to hallucinate things? I haven't changed the doses on any of my meds lately, but I slept horribly. I think I'm just suffering from severe sleep deprivation.

Maybe I need to lay off the coffee. Try some warm milk at night before bedtime.

Blech. I should talk to my doctor about sleeping pills. I've read that not getting enough sleep can lead to memory loss. And I don't want the nightmares to be the only thing I remember about my sister. I don't want to forget the good Iris memories, of staying up late together on Christmas Eve or sharing birthday cakes or when she held my hand on the first day of kindergarten. Or the time I held her hand on the first day of seventh grade.

I pull a long-sleeved pink shirt out of the back of the closet. This would surprise Trista and Natalie, along with most of my school. Would they think I'm trying to dress like my sister?

Then again, the pale pink shirt does say, "On Wednesdays We Wear Black." It's from the last season of *American Horror Story,* a show Iris and I watched together. She liked horror movies even more than I do. I decide to wear the shirt, not to pretend to be Iris, but because it makes me remember good things about her. Happy things.

I know Mom hopes one day I'll dress more like her friends' daughters, more like Iris. But I'm comfortable in my clothes. And it's not like I have strange piercings or tattoos or wear vampire contacts. Iris never got yelled at for wearing trampy short shorts and halter tops around the house, but the moment I wear a very proper, skin-covering black hoodie with sugar skulls, I get pained looks and am kidnapped to the department store for an armload of pastel polo shirts.

Goth rehab.

It's chilly enough this morning that I end up covering the pink shirt with my sugar skull hoodie. Maybe I won't be brave today. Even if I tell myself I'm not being chicken. It's just that I don't want to deal with people staring at me. I don't like the extra attention.

But I can still think of Iris and the night we binge watched the first two seasons of *American Horror Story* and made ourselves sick with kettle corn.

I keep my pink secret through first and second block and even when it gets warm in third block because Mrs. Davis cranks her heater up. She is a frail, gray-haired little thing who has no body heat of her own. So the rest of us must suffer and smell each other's sweat while she teaches. This is another reason why I fall asleep in algebra.

My heart tingles in my chest when I see that someone has answered my Christina Rossetti with more Rossetti. From the same poem, actually. Just two lines.

> *I strain my heart, I stretch my hands,*
> *And catch at hope*

He knows. This definitely means he knows. I think. My head swims. Or possibly swoons. I could so easily fall in love with this boy. But I know that would be dangerous. *He's not for you,* I tell myself. He never was. It's best that I erase the words and focus on trinomials and such.

I promise myself I'll erase it at the end of class. I'm too busy admiring the penmanship. His *a*'s are printed while the rest of his letters are a sharp but neat cursive. It's definitely the handwriting of an artist. A dreamer.

My mind goes blank as I try to think of another poem. The bell rings, and I still don't have anything to write. With a sigh, I erase his words. Maybe I'm reading things into these lines that aren't really there.

At lunch, I sit with Natalie and Trista in the quad, keeping an eye out for Alex. His friends aren't out here, so I wonder if they are skipping today. I can't ask Trista about them, though, without her asking a million questions.

But a fight breaks out on the far side of the courtyard. Thing Two and someone I don't recognize. A senior, I think. After a lot of screaming and hollering, the fight is broken up and the two boys are taken to the principal's office to wait for the police. Our school has a zero tolerance policy. You get in a fight, you go to jail.

Hank appears behind us, apparently pretending he had nothing to do with the altercation. He puts one arm around Natalie and the other around me. "Who's going to come see us play Saturday night at Lucy's?"

I pluck his arm off of me. "Sorry. Too busy watching paint dry."

"Ouch," Hank says. "Ladies?" He moves his hands to Trista's shoulders, massaging her neck in an almost NC-17 way. "You should all be there. I've asked Pluto to bring the good organic shit his friend from rehab makes."

That swoony, fluttery feeling I had in my chest earlier this morning is gone, replaced by cold lead. How could I be so stupid to believe Alex could change?

"I assume you're talking about some awesome organic coffee," I say. There's the tiniest possibility I'm jumping to conclusions.

Hank laughs at me. "You are adorable. Marry me."

Trista turns around and slaps him on the arm. "Ass hat."

"Hey. Zero tolerance, remember?" Natalie says, nodding toward the assistant principal, who is still talking to the teacher who was on duty out here when the fight broke out.

Hank smirks at Trista. "Come home with me and you can beat me all you want."

"Ugh," Trista says.

"Besides, we have soccer practice today," Natalie adds. "No beatings for you. What was that fight about?"

Hank shrugs. "Caleb didn't like something that guy said."

Natalie's eyes get huge. "Really? What did he say to him?"

But Hank won't elaborate and the bell rings and we have to go to English. I hear snippets of rumors in the halls about the fight, but no one knows what happened, other than the fact that both boys were taken away in handcuffs in the back of a cop car.

Mr. Herrington proclaims today a silent reading period, but I can't concentrate on the book I have. Natalie has given me a light paranormal romance from her locker. It's cute, but I get more and more agitated as I wait for the end of school. If Alex wasn't here at lunch, he probably won't show up in the library this afternoon. This is a good thing. I'm sure I can get much more work done without him there to distract me.

CHAPTER 11

Dammit.

Alex is already sitting in the library when I get there. I ignore him and go up to Verla's desk. I pull the astronomy journal out of my bag and slide it back to her. "Thanks for letting me borrow this."

She grins. "Did you replace your eyepiece yet?"

"No," I say, avoiding Alex's gaze. "I found a used one on eBay for about a hundred dollars. But I never bothered to tell my parents I broke it."

"But accidents happen," Verla says. "Surely they'll understand. Is your birthday coming up soon?"

I shake my head. "September." At least that's closer than Christmas.

"Did you see the full moon last night? It was gorgeous, even without a telescope," Verla says. "Right around ten, ten thirty, there was a bright star just below it, over in the western sky. Do you know what star that was? Or was it a planet? Or a comet, maybe?"

"Jupiter," I say. I did get a glance at him last night before I went to sleep.

"Cool!" Verla beams. "I knew you'd know."

I haven't told her about my plans for the Lyrid shower. It's going to be tricky enough sneaking out of the house and driving somewhere out of the city where the sky is dark enough to see the meteors. There are no true dark skies over Georgia, but GSU's astronomy department has an observatory in a state park less than an hour south of here. I've been to the observatory once on a field trip in elementary school, and I think I can drive there easily at night.

The best part is that Mom and Craig have a home builders convention in Atlanta that week. Grandma Lydia is supposed to come and stay with me that week, to make sure I take my medicine and don't fall in the shower and don't sneak boys into the house. And Grandma Lydia has sharper hearing than anyone else I know in my family. But she also goes to bed early and rises before five. I'll be back home long before then.

I sit down and start working on the stack of poetry books, not saying anything to Alex. He is busy texting on his phone and not doing his work. But Verla doesn't seem to notice.

I finish cataloging a book of Charles Bukowski, then two collections of Elizabeth Barrett Browning, while Alex continues to text. I read a biography about Browning once and learned she was an invalid for most of her life, with some strange malady that the doctors of her time could not diagnose. I wonder if she had seizures.

Alex sighs, frustrated at something, and throws his phone down on the desk. He grabs a book and slams it down next to his computer, opening it to the title page.

I glance over at the book's title. "What did Miss Emily ever do to you?"

He shoves the book away. "That goth chick just depresses me with her imaginary love affairs."

I can't let him get away with insulting Emily Dickinson. Even if her poems are depressing. I glare at him. "You're putting those labels on wrong. They won't scan properly that way."

"Don't be mental," Alex snarls.

"Don't be an ass hat." I cringe at my not-so-sparkling wit. And having to steal insults from Tris.

Alex does not answer, ignoring me as he catalogs the Emily Dickinson book into the system. He remains silent as he slams the book shut and grabs another one.

"Someone like you just wouldn't get poems by someone like her."

"Someone like me? What makes you think you know me?" he asks quietly.

There's more bitterness in his voice now than I've ever heard before. "What makes you think I don't?" I continue to amaze myself at my own sheer lack of cleverness.

Alex seems unimpressed. "For starters, I am not falling off the wagon, despite what everyone is saying. I do not smoke, drink, snort, or ingest any illegal substance anymore. I'm clean."

"Then why did you start in the first place?" If only he'd been sober last year, maybe my sister would still be here.

He rubs his forehead. "Because I thought it was what I needed to do. Because I thought that was how all the good songwriters get inspired."

I can only stare at him as he bares his soul to me. It makes me feel imposed upon. I really don't want to know him any more than I already do. "That is the stupidest thing I've ever heard."

"Would it be more acceptable to you if I said my dad never loved me and my moms beat the shit out of me? That I never had a normal childhood and sought love in the bottom of a bottle of rum?"

I roll my eyes. "Sounds more likely." But now I'm not so sure. And I can't keep myself from asking, "Did you really think you could be the next John Lennon by getting high or drunk?"

He shrugs and stares at the pen he is tapping against the table. "That's the way my dad does it."

"Your dad is a musician too?" I don't know why this astonishes me. It's like he just opened the door to a strange and mysterious place. Alexland. No wonder everyone calls him Pluto.

"I used to spend my summers with him and his wife in Memphis. Until the social worker found out they were letting me smoke pot." He looks over at me, and I swear the sneer on his face makes him look like a demonic Elvis. "And what were you doing the summer you were twelve? Going to Six Flags with your perfect family and sharing secrets with your sister? Because your life was perfect before I came and turned your sister into a drug addict, right?"

"No, but we were happy enough. And we didn't go to Six Flags. We went to Disney World."

He doesn't answer. He picks up another book and starts typing again. Every few minutes, he stops to check something on his phone.

I know I should leave him alone. I should go back to my own pile of books and focus on finishing today's work. The book I pick up next is an Amy Lowell collection. I flip through it and my eyes fall upon "Fireworks."

> You hate me and I hate you,
> And we are so polite, we two!
>
> But whenever I see you, I burst apart
> And scatter the sky with my blazing heart.
> In spits and sparkles in stars and balls,
> Buds into roses—and flares, and falls.

I want to giggle. What would he think if he found this on the desk in Mrs. Davis's class tomorrow? He'd know who his fellow vandal was for certain. If he hasn't already guessed.

But do we actually hate each other? I glance over at him as he scowls at his phone.

I have no idea how he feels about me, but yes, I can definitely say I hate Alex Hammond.

CHAPTER 12

Trista and Natalie are leaving soccer practice, when my library work is finished. Natalie waves as they both wander over to where I'm waiting for my mom. Craig had to meet with builders in Atlanta this afternoon, so they must have practiced without him. It would have been nice to bum a ride home with him, instead of waiting out here where I might run into Alex again.

"We're going to Rock 'n' Roll Graveyard tomorrow night," Natalie says, still bouncing with energy even after two hours of chasing a ball across a field. "And you are coming with us."

"I am?"

She nods. "No excuses this time. You need to get out and socialize more. You're wasting away inside that dark and scary library."

I shrug. "They have fluorescent lights. And sometimes Verla feeds us."

"Us?" Trista asks. "Who all's serving time with you?"

I groan. I'll never hear the end of it once they find out.

Alex comes out the front door and actually runs into Natalie on his way to the parking lot.

"Ouch!" she says, rubbing her arm.

Trista's eyes grow huge as we all stare at him, stalking off without saying a word to any of us. He heads off campus toward Broad Street. He must be walking to his moms' café.

"Mr. I'm-Hot-but-Anti-Social-in-a-Not-So-Adorable-Way?" she asks, looking back at me.

I shrug. "We have settled into a comfortably frosty working relationship. He doesn't talk to me and I don't talk to him. It works. Anyway, I thought it wasn't safe to go to the Graveyard anymore."

Trista smiles. "They put up a few more 'No Trespassing' signs and some yellow tape, but you can still get over the fence."

The abandoned private cemetery used to be a popular spot for bringing dates and booze. Part of the thrill is the possibility you will hear or see one of the alleged ghosts. Or possibly even cops. Certainly not the tribe of albinos the older kids used to tell us lived out there.

Supposedly a singer from a 1950s band who was caught cheating with his manager's wife shot himself and was buried in this cemetery. On hot summer nights, they say you can hear him singing. Or you might see an Indian princess whose tribe was massacred on this land by a warring tribe.

I shake my head. "I don't think my mom will let me go out."

"She will if she thinks you're spending the night with me," Natalie says. "My mom already asked your mom."

"And does your mom know we're going to the cemetery?" I ask.

"Of course not. She thinks we're going to see Calcifer play."

I want to roll my eyes again, but my head is starting to hurt. "Anything but that."

Natalie giggles. "They're not that bad."

She's right. The one time I did see one of their shows, Cal-cifer kinda rocked. But they were all stoned and only sounded good when they were playing their own stuff. Alex's stuff.

Trista jumps up as her older sister pulls into the circle in front of the school. "Come on, Webb. You can ride with us."

"My mom is coming," I say. "But thanks."

"See you tomorrow." Trista opens the passenger door of her sister's red Firebird, and Natalie pulls the seat forward to squeeze into the back. Her sister doesn't wave or say hi. She's busy yelling at someone on her cell phone. She is in the nursing program at the local junior college. She is even more of a bitch than Trista.

Mom pulls up not long after Trista and Natalie leave. I'm careful not to let my backpack look too heavy. She looks tired and is trying to get hold of Craig on her cell phone.

Giving up, she pushes the button to disconnect. "How was your day?"

"Fine, how was yours?" I ask.

"Busy. I worked through lunch so I'm starving. I thought we'd eat out since it's just the two of us tonight. Have a girls' night out." She smiles at me hopefully.

"Sounds good. What are you craving?" I ask. "Thai?"

She shakes her head. "Had Thai yesterday for lunch. I keep hearing good things about that Indigo Dragon café over by Broad. My secretary said they have wonderful vegetarian burg-ers. How about we try that?"

My appetite disappears. And it's not because she wants me to eat tofu. She doesn't know about the Hammonds.

The Indigo is not far from our school, and she's already pulling in to one of the parking spaces near the front door. She was lucky getting the spot. It looks like they're busy, and it's not even six thirty yet.

She notices my lack of enthusiasm, and her face falls as she turns off the engine. "Or you could get a regular hamburger, if you wanted. Or we can just get takeout if you're not feeling up to it."

"Mom, that's not it. Alex Hammond's parents own this café."

Her hands fall from the steering wheel to her lap. "Oh."

She's silent for several moments. She stares straight ahead, because I've reminded her of the daughter she lost all over again. Why didn't I keep my mouth shut?

"Do you think his parents will be here? They wouldn't come out of the kitchen and try to talk to us, would they?"

Oh dear lord. "Mom, Alex works at the counter. *He* would have to talk to us." Then again, with the mood he was in earlier today, maybe he wouldn't.

"That boy doesn't bother you at school, does he?"

I want to laugh. "No. We leave each other alone. I pretend he doesn't exist and he pretends I don't exist."

"Why would you bother him?"

I stare at her. "Well, I do kinda look like his dead girlfriend."

She sighs and turns the engine back on. "I guess we can just make sandwich wraps at home. I think there's still some tuna fish in the fridge."

Ick. "No, wait," I say. "What if we go to the Mexican place across the street? They used to have really good nachos."

She glances across the street at Lupita's Taqueria. "I suppose. I could go for some veggie quesadillas."

"Great." I hop out of the car before she changes her mind. I know it's a minute possibility, but what if Alex sees us outside and thinks I asked my mom to bring me here?

I hurry her across the street, dodging traffic. I don't feel safe until we're inside Lupita's and a smiling Lupita herself is seating us in a secluded booth in the back, near the mariachi band.

Mom lets me eat most of the chips and salsa, and orders a

quesadilla with grilled zucchini and mushrooms. She frowns when I order a Diet Coke instead of water, but says nothing when I get the grilled shrimp fajitas.

"You really have to watch the chemicals you put in your body," she says, when Lupita takes our menus away. "I've read all sorts of horrible things about aspartame. It's poison."

I shrug and reach for another chip. It's warm in here, so I take off my hoodie, and Mom looks amazed to see the pink shirt I've been hiding underneath.

She doesn't mention it, but I can tell she's pleased. "And the aluminum in the cans isn't good for you either. At least drink your poison out of a glass."

I grin. "Of course."

She takes her phone out of her purse and tries calling Craig again. He's supposed to be coming back tomorrow from his business trip.

She puts the phone down on the table and stabs a chip into the salsa. "That idiot must have forgotten his charger again. Why wouldn't he let me pack for him? Ooh, this is spicy!"

I grin at her as she reaches for her water glass. And I realize we're both having fun, for the first time in forever. And it feels . . . nice.

"Thanks for taking me out tonight," I tell her. "I can't remember the last time we came here."

Mom smiles back at me, but her smile grows fragile. "We were here after Iris's team won the district all-stars game last spring."

Crap. I wish I hadn't made her remember that. "They beat Augusta Prep."

Fortunately Lupita brings our food to the table, but not before Mom grows melancholy again. I know it's okay to miss Iris. And Mom knows it's okay to talk about her. But I think we're alike in that we don't like too many icky emotions.

Crying is exhausting. And I've cried so much for my sister that I feel drained. I can't let go of the grief, but I've got to make room inside me for some other emotions too. And right now, watching Mom eat spicy salsa makes me feel happy. Even if just for the moment. And being happy just for one moment is enough for now. It means maybe there will be other chances for more happiness in the future.

I don't think Mom sees it that way. Her smile is already gone, and she is back in fierce Momma Bear mode. Don't let your guard down. Don't make a mistake and let another cub fall into harm's way.

I curl my fingers around my glass of Diet Coke defensively.

But she only puts her napkin in her lap, staring at her plate without really looking at the food.

"This looks wonderful," I say. "Craig will be jealous when he finds out we went here without him."

She picks up her fork and knife to cut her quesadilla into tiny pieces instead of using her hands. "Oh, I'm sure he's wining and dining those contractors in Atlanta at someplace fancy. I talked with Natalie's mother today. I told her I was fine with you sleeping over with Natalie tomorrow night if you want to go. Just remember to take your medicine before bedtime and don't stay up too late."

I start to tell her I don't feel like going, but she really wants me to start being sociable again. And so do my friends.

I give in. "I will. Thanks for letting me go."

She gives me another almost smile, and it's worth suffering through a miserable night trying to socialize with stoned and/or drunk classmates. I can't believe I can rationalize it that way.

We are pulling into the garage when Craig finally returns Mom's call. I grab my backpack out of the car and go on into the house, not wanting to hear their conversation. Not because it will be intimate and NC-17 rated, but because it will be boring and business related. I have a ton of chemistry homework to do anyway.

I'm falling asleep on my open book when my phone vibrates on my desk.

"Meet me outside."

It's not a number that's programmed into my phone, but I still recognize it. Alex. No "please," no polite request for the pleasure of my company. I roll my eyes, but curiosity gets the better of me. I pull a black hoodie on over my tank top and pray he doesn't say anything about my cupcake pajama pants.

I can hear Mom's raised voice coming from her bedroom. "Are you out of your mind? We can't afford that right now."

I hurry down the hallway to the front of the house. I don't want to know what Craig's bought now, but he likes his toys. A boat. A motorcycle. His convertible. Even if Mom nags and worries, his real estate business is doing well.

"Why couldn't you wait to discuss this with me when you're home?"

I open the front door as quietly as possible and slip out onto the porch.

Alex is sitting on our porch swing, with something in his hands.

I walk over toward him but don't sit down with him. I cross my arms. It's cold out here, and my ankles are freezing.

"This is for you." Alex hands me what looks like a crumpled-up grocery bag, but something heavy is inside.

I unwrap it carefully. A Celestron Barlow lens. I look up at Alex in shock.

"It was the 3x version that you had, right?" he asks. "The one that broke?"

"Just the 2x."

He shrugs, shoving his hands in his jacket pockets. He's wearing that army surplus jacket that makes him look like one of the surgeons from *MASH*. "Well, you just got an upgrade."

I'm so astonished, I forget my manners. "Where did you find this? How much was it?"

"I found it in the pawn shop over by the university. And it's not polite to ask someone how much they paid for something they're giving you."

"But, you shouldn't be giving me a gift," I say stupidly. "I was saving up for this. Or for one like it. You shouldn't have . . . wait, what did you pawn to get this?"

Alex sighs. "Jesus." He stands up and starts to leave, taking the porch steps two at a time.

"Wait." I reach out and manage to grab his sleeve before he leaves. "I'm sorry, Alex. Thank you. You didn't have to do it, but thank you."

He shrugs my hand away, but turns at the bottom of the steps, looking up at me. "It was my fault. I've been trying to order one since last week, when your other lens broke. But first I had to figure out what exactly I'd broken. And where I was going to get one. And if I was mad today in the library, it was because I'd been waiting for the guy at the pawn shop to call me back. I didn't want you thinking you'd have to replace it yourself."

"You went to all that trouble for me?" I stare at the lens in my hand, still dazed by this strange but kind person that looks like Alex Hammond. "Are you a nice alien that stole Alex's body? And you want me to help you phone home?"

He looks like he wants to laugh. Almost. "Don't get any crazy ideas. I'm still not a nice person."

"Of course not." But something in my chest believes otherwise.

"This was just a debt of honor."

"Okay."

"I felt bad about breaking your other one and you not being able to see your stars. It was weighing on my conscience."

"Thank you, Alex."

"You're welcome." He turns to go.

I have a crazy urge to hug him, or kiss him on the cheek. But it seems like a flirty thing to do. Not an Andria thing to do. I'm not a flirty person.

I watch him walk back down the sidewalk, hands still in his pockets. I don't say anything, and don't try to stop him. I cradle the lens close to me, like it's a newborn kitten, and watch until he disappears from my view down the street and heads back to his house.

CHAPTER 13

Eight Days

Mom left a large cooler packed full of nutritious snacks for me in the fridge to take to Natalie's tonight. Carrot sticks and hummus. Granola bars. An apple and a pear. Six bottles of water and a freezer pack to keep them chilled. Mom knows Natalie's mom is a pastry chef and is probably worried that Mrs. Roman plans to feed us nothing but buttercream all weekend.

Not that I would object. Mrs. Roman's French Toast Maple Bacon cupcakes are sinfully good. Natalie's mom is picking us all up from school, so I have to drag the health food rations and my backpack stuffed with overnight essentials from class to class today. I probably won't have any granola bars left by the end of fourth block.

Mom was also nice enough to drop me off at school this morning, so I wouldn't have to cart all this crap on the bus. I still feel like a bag lady. Trista and Hank are kind enough to relieve me of the cooler. They are apparently "on" again, by the way their lips keep bumping into each other.

It's kind of chilly this morning, and the sky is a dark, dolphin-belly gray. Looks like rain again. I hope against hope that tonight's outing to the wilderness will be canceled and we'll spend the night in the Roman family's den instead, watching Netflix movies and eating cupcakes.

"Brrr! Fuck, it's cold!" Trista says, hopping up and down as she rummages through my health food stash. Hank grabs for the hummus, but she smacks his hand. "Not for you. Here, have an apple."

He takes the apple and runs off.

Trista hands the cooler back to me. "So you're really hanging out with us tonight."

"Looks like it," I say.

She looks up at me and grins. "This is going to be awesome. Nat, who do you think we should hook her up with?"

Natalie takes a step back to examine me critically, but I shake my head. "There will be no hooking tonight. Not for me."

Natalie giggles. "Tris, you know better. Andria is not into hooking."

"No hooking up, no hooking down, not even hooking sideways?" Trista asks, still grinning.

"Definitely not sideways," I say, and they both laugh as Alex Hammond walks past us with Erin Young, a sophomore on the soccer team. She waves to Trista and Natalie with a friendly smile.

"Did you see . . . ?" a bewildered Natalie trails off, as Trista's jaw drops inelegantly.

I am too busy examining with mild astonishment how upset this is making me. Erin is sweet and cute, and it makes perfect sense that Alex needs a new girlfriend who is nothing like Iris. Erin is innocent. Erin does not take drugs. Erin is so effing healthy she has a rosy glow in her cheeks. Erin wears frilly skirts when she is not on the soccer field.

He is going to corrupt her. Steal her innocence.

Or, she might be able to save him.

And a wicked little thought floats through my brain. Why can't that be me?

Wait, did I really just think that?

"Since when?" Trista murmurs. "I thought she was dating that boy from Athens Prep."

Natalie shrugs. "I think her dad has a law office close to the Indigo Dragon."

That does not mean they have enough in common to start dating.

Ugh. I cannot look like this is upsetting to me.

"And I thought he wasn't over Iris," Natalie says sadly.

Right. Iris is the reason he shouldn't be dating Erin Young. Not me. He should still be getting over Iris. I slip into ice-queen mode and shrug. "It's not like he and Iris were that serious. They only dated for what, three or four months? It's been longer than that since she died. That's hardly a love to end all loves."

Natalie and Trista look at each other. Trista is frowning.

"It wasn't like a Princess Leia–Han Solo love," I add, trying not to sound so ice queenish.

They both laugh as the bell rings. "I guess you're right," Natalie says, and puts her arm around me. "Were you always such a cold-hearted cynic?"

I shrug and let them lead me into chemistry.

Trista turns around as soon as she slides into her seat. "Hey, I'm calling the north corner tonight."

Natalie pouts. "You always get that corner. No fair."

The north corner of Rock 'n' Roll Graveyard is the darkest side. There's a bench hidden from the rest of the cemetery by a Spanish moss–covered camellia bush. The perfect spot for making out.

I play with Natalie's red curls that are lying on my desk. "And just who do you think you'd take into the corner with you, young lady?"

She blushes, and her cheeks turn as red as her hair. "Oh, I don't know. Maybe Thomas. He and Sara only went out on two or three dates and she dumped him for Max."

"Poor Thomas," I say. "But what about Thing Two?"

"Caleb?" She looks at me, surprised, but I'm not sure why. She went out with him last summer, and they are still friendly. I've seen her gaze at him longingly, wistfully even. "Andria, if you're interested in him, you should go for it!"

"Oh my God, no."

She tucks a curl behind her ear. "Seriously, he's an octopus, but go. Have fun with him. Tris, you'll have to give up the corner. We're going to hook her up with Caleb."

"Please, no. Seriously. I thought you still had feelings for him. Besides, didn't he get suspended for that fight yesterday? Did we ever find out what that was all about?"

Tris leans around Natalie. "Hank said he had no idea."

Natalie takes a deep breath, about to say something more, but the teacher begins to call roll. All during class, Trista and Natalie keep looking at me and giggling. They are making Plans for Andria.

Maybe I will get lucky and be hit by a car before fourth block.

There is no poetry on my desk today in algebra. I'm not surprised, and I keep telling myself I shouldn't be disappointed. What if he thought he was writing to Erin all this time? She probably has Mrs. Davis for geometry. He's been writing to the wrong girl all along. Or maybe the wrong girl has been writing him back.

I'm so depressed I eat all of my hummus at lunch. I go to the library before fourth block to tell Verla I can't stay after school today since I have to ride home with Natalie's mom.

I really don't want to see Alex anyway.

Verla is happy to see me. "Thank goodness! I was going to

send you a message next period to tell you I have to leave right after school. Can you tell Alex?"

I shake my head. "I usually don't see him until we come here. I have no idea what he has for fourth block."

"Oh well. I guess I'll get the secretary to tell him. Have a good weekend," she says.

"You too."

I should not be depressed over having to miss my library work. That would just be lame. But I am. Even though I have something even more exciting tonight that I should be looking forward to.

But I'm too worried about tonight to be excited. I'm scared I might have a seizure in front of everyone. I'm scared my dog will get lonely tonight without me. I'm scared one of my friends will party too hard and something bad will happen.

I'm scared I'll see Alex tonight and say something stupid.

I'm scared I won't see him.

CHAPTER 14

After school, Natalie's mom picks up Natalie, Trista, and me in a gray Suburban that smells like vanilla cupcakes. She still thinks we are going to the coffeehouse on Broad Street to see our friends' band play. Trista's sister and her boyfriend are going to pick us up at eight.

"I want you guys to be my guinea pigs tonight," Mrs. Roman says. "I made Cherry Coke float cupcakes. I want to know what you think."

"What about real food?" Natalie asks. I can't believe her. If my mom were a pastry chef, I'd eat cupcakes for breakfast, lunch, and dinner.

"Pizza from Tony's."

Natalie grins. "Best mom ever."

The Romans live in one of the newer neighborhoods close to the river. Their two-story house makes me nervous, and my mother's safety rules echo in my head. *Always take the elevator—if you have a seizure you could fall down the stairs and break your neck.* As if I couldn't trip over my feet on the ground and break my neck just as easily. I have never been very graceful or athletic, thanks to Mom refusing to let me play sports or take ballet lessons.

It's really too bad the Romans don't have an elevator.

The garage door opens, and Mrs. Roman pulls in. Natalie hops out and helps me carry my stuff inside. My lunch cooler is already empty. Time for some real food.

"Tris, I thought your goal last week against Academy was amazing," Mrs. Roman is telling Trista as they follow us into the house.

"Thanks. I wish my parents had been there to see it." There's bitterness in her voice, but it's mild. Like she's finally resigned herself to the fact that they don't come to her soccer games.

The kitchen smells heavenly. Like basil and oregano and tomato sauce. My stomach is growling. And I don't care if anyone hears it.

"The pizza is in the oven on warm," Mrs. Roman says. "Go dump your things in Natalie's room and it will be waiting for you when you're ready."

"Thanks, Mom," Natalie says, already halfway up the stairs.

I follow her carefully, with Trista right behind me. I try to move to let her pass.

"Are you afraid of heights?" she asks. The staircase is an open metal one, spiraling up the enormous foyer.

"No, just afraid of falling."

She laughs and runs up ahead of me. Her laugh echoes across the huge cold space.

I take a deep breath and hurry after her. I've been to Natalie's house millions of times, and I'm fine once I'm inside her bedroom. But this staircase always freaks me out.

One step at a time. Focus on the top, Andria. Breathe in, breathe out.

Natalie's head appears at the railing. "Yoooou can doooo

eeet!" she says. "Or do you want me to come down and get your things?"

"No, I'm almost there."

She waits patiently for me to reach the second floor, and takes my backpack. "What are you wearing tonight?"

Trista is already stripped out of her school clothes and rummaging through Natalie's closet. "Where is that green sleeveless thing, Nat? The one you wore to the movies?"

"God, it's too cold for that," Natalie says. "I'm wearing stockings under my jeans."

"We're supposed to be going to a concert where there will be dancing. You'll look suspicious if you're dressed for an outing in the snow."

"And you will get hypothermia if you wear that top."

Natalie pushes Trista out of the way playfully and disappears into her enormous closet.

"Andria, this is what you should wear tonight. It would go great with your hair."

She comes out holding up a purple silk peasant blouse with smocked flowers. Iris loved this top and begged Natalie over and over to let her wear it.

"I can't," I say, even though I want to. It's a dark jewel-toned purple. Amethyst. And she's right, it would be perfect with my black hair. But it's not perfect for me. It would have been perfect for Iris. I turn to my bag and dig through it. "I have a top. It's warm and cozy. . . ."

"And black?" Trista says.

"Of course." I pull the long-sleeved shirt out and hold it up. It has tiny skull-shaped buttons up the front. Very feminine.

Natalie busts out laughing. "Fine. But you're going to wear some color at some point this year, if it kills me."

I turn around and freeze, but she's already skipping down the stairs.

Trista looks at me uncomfortably. I shake my head. I have to stop being so sensitive. People joke about death. Because people die every day. And I have to get used to that.

I step into Natalie's closet to change my shirt.

"You know she didn't mean anything by it, right?" Trista asks.

"Yes. I'm okay. I promise." Still, it surprises me she's that concerned. I guess she really did feel bad after saying those things about Iris the other day. "I'll be down in a second," I tell her. "You don't have to wait."

I poke my head out to see that she's already gone. I have to laugh at myself for assuming she'd wait. It's really not all about me. The world is going to go right on spinning, whether I want it to stop or not. Sisters die. Boys fall in love. Friends move on.

I glance at myself in the mirror: a pale, black-haired girl with shadows under her eyes. Great, I really do look like I belong in a graveyard.

I paw through Natalie's makeup bag and find a dark red lipstick. There, now I have some color.

Trista and Natalie both love it. I find them sitting at the bar in the Romans' kitchen, eating pizza. "You look like a vampire!" Trista cackles.

She still insists on wearing the sleeveless top tonight, even though Natalie and I both know she's going to freeze.

Natalie has changed into a pale pink sweater that goes great with her red curls. She has a purple striped scarf hanging around her neck. She slides a plate with a piece of pizza across the bar toward me. "There are drinks in the fridge. Help yourself."

Trista texts her sister, to remind her of Natalie's address. "Her boyfriend doesn't get off work until nine, so he's going to meet us there."

"Is he bringing," Natalie whispers as she looks around to make sure her mom is not close by, "the rum?"

Trista nods.

I roll my eyes.

Natalie looks from me to Trista with the biggest smile and a tiny squee. "This is going to be so much fun!"

Trista is looking at me as if she does not believe I will have any fun.

Natalie looks at her phone, and her smile gets even bigger. "Tris, you may only have the dark corner for one hour. After ten, it's mine."

I gesture at her phone with what's left of my slice of pizza. "Thomas?"

"Maybe." Her cheeks match her sweater. She types something back and puts her phone away.

Trista gets up and takes her empty plate to the sink. "Come on, girls. We need to finish getting ready. Selena will be here in less than an hour."

The knot of worry in my stomach has been there all day, but now it's growing worse. I worry about my friends. They know not to pressure me to drink or take drugs. Not only because of Iris, but also because they know my seizure meds do not play well with alcohol or other drugs. Especially after the wine cooler incident. But I don't think they know how nervous I get watching them drink. I'm so scared something bad will happen to one of them.

CHAPTER 15

This sucks. Selena has already left us, and while I worry about how we'll get home, Natalie and Thomas are making out in the Dark Corner and Trista and Hank are making out Right in Front of Me. I have seen parts of Trista's body I have no business seeing.

And I am out of Diet Coke.

I stare into the flames of the bonfire Thing One and Thing Two have lit. Caleb looked a little forlorn when he saw Natalie and Thomas disappear holding hands, but after a six-pack of beer, he tried pawing at me. I shoved him off, and he slunk over to the other side of the fire, where a few other girls from the soccer team were giggling and drinking. They seem more than happy to help comfort him.

Another pair of headlights swings into the gravel drive that circles the fenced property. A large white truck. Oh God, no.

Alex gets out of the truck and walks over to where I'm standing. He leans up against the fence with me, his hands in the pockets of his army-green jacket. What I wouldn't give to have a jacket right now. Even standing this close to the bonfire, my backside is freezing.

"Pluto!" Caleb shouts from across the flames. He raises his bottle in a salute, and the girls hanging on him giggle.

I don't look up at Alex, but I can tell he's tense. What does he have to be uptight about? And why is he standing next to me? "Hank said you were bringing the good stuff. Fall off the wagon already?"

Suddenly he is right in front of me, his tall frame shading me from the firelight. "What are you talking about?"

I want to step back but there's no room. I try not to look intimidated. Instead I glare at him. I don't say anything.

"And why the hell are you hanging out with such lowly company, Cupcake? Did you come to drink and smoke your cares away?"

"Don't be ridiculous."

"Don't make assumptions about people you don't understand."

"You still think I don't understand you?"

His blue eyes seem to glow when he smiles. But his smile isn't friendly. It makes me wonder what a genuine smile would look like on his face. "No, you don't." He stalks off toward Caleb and the soccer girls. Erin is over there and smiles when Alex reaches them. But he doesn't take the beer she offers him. Nor does he let her touch his hair, or stand too close to him. I watch as he dodges her touchy-feely hands but still laughs and cuts up with Caleb.

Trista looks up at me from the ground, where she's been rolling with Hank. "Honey, did you see Nathan over by the crypt? He was hoping you'd be here tonight."

Nathan wears head-to-toe black and has hair blacker than mine. He also wears eyeliner. I roll my eyes as Hank giggles and adds, "He said—"

Trista slaps him and shrieks. "No! Don't tell her what he said!"

Hank is still laughing. "He said he'd be happy to stake you with his—"

"You dumb-ass!" Trista says. "She won't go near him now." She is giggling too. Hilarious.

Hank waves to Caleb. "Come on, I need another drink," he says, tugging Trista along with him. She stumbles after him toward the other side of the bonfire.

Someone taps me on the shoulder, and I whip around, expecting Nathan and his Jonathan Harker fetish. "Leave me alone!" I snap.

A startled Alex is standing there, holding a can of Diet Coke in each hand. "Peace offering. I thought you looked thirsty."

Every time I think I have him figured out, Alex does something nice and tilts the universe a little bit.

He gently clinks his can against the one I'm now holding in my hand. "Cheers." He cracks open the can and takes a sip, making a face. "God, this stuff tastes better with Crown."

I roll my eyes at him, but I am grateful for the drink. I'm starting to worry about Nat. She and Thomas should have been back from the corner long ago. "If you don't like it, then give it here."

He pulls his can back, just out of my reach. "Nope. Need the caffeine."

I look up at Alex. Really look at him. He's watching his friends on the other side of the bonfire. "Are you really not drinking alcohol tonight?"

His concerned gaze settles on me. "I can't go back to that life anymore." He frowns as he looks at the crowd gathered around the fire. "But it's so hard."

"I know." But I don't know. I've never struggled with addiction. Never known how it felt to crave something so violently that I thought I couldn't live without it. Would lie, cheat, or steal to have it. Just how much of an addict was Alex? I only saw him high that one night.

But then again, I'd never actually seen my sister high either. Hungover, yes. Tipsy after a date with Alex, yes. Coming down on Monday morning, God yes. But she never actually got high around me. Whatever her reasons for using drugs, she kept them hidden.

I glance around the clearing, seeing only a lot of drunk, horny teenagers. No, two seniors whose names I don't remember get out of a van they've been sitting in, their eyes red. It's not long before we can all smell the pot.

Police in Atlanta can probably smell it.

Beside me, Alex tenses again.

"Why are you here tonight?" he asks. "You don't look like you're having fun."

Neither does he, actually. I shrug. "I'm watching out for my friends. I want to make sure no one gets hurt."

"Andria." Alex says my name so softly, so sadly, I'm forced to look up at him. "You can't save everyone." He moves away from the fence and holds out a hand. "Come on, we need to get out of here."

I'm not about to take his hand. He shrugs and puts his hands back in his pockets as I just glare at him. Natalie and Thomas have reappeared from their turn in the Dark Corner of the cemetery and are laughing with Nathan and his friends. Trista is leading Hank by his shirt collar back to the corner for their second turn. All friends present and accounted for.

I follow Alex back across the clearing and through the open gate to where he is parked.

He opens the door to his truck for me. "Come on. Neither one of us belongs here."

He's right. But I don't think I belong in his truck, alone with him, either. "Give me a ride home?" I ask.

"Aren't you supposed to be spending the night with Natalie?"

He's right. If I go home now, I could get Natalie into trouble for this. And Trista. I climb into the front seat, and he shuts the door.

I wait for him to get in on his side and take a deep breath. At least it's warm in the truck. But there's not a lot of air in here once he's inside the space with me. And the truck smells like Alex. Like apple-scented shampoo and fresh-baked bread from the Indigo Dragon. "Okay," I say, trying hard not to panic. "What do we do now?"

His hands are on the steering wheel. "I have no clue."

His honesty makes me want to giggle. And then I embarrass myself by yawning.

"Tired?"

I could fall asleep right here, but I can't let him know that. This is weird. The Alex air that I'm breathing in is just too much. It suffocates me. I need outside air. Normal air. I open the truck door.

"What's wrong?" Alex asks.

"I'm getting claustrophobic," I say. But as I look out across Rock 'n' Roll Graveyard, I don't want to go back there either.

"I have an idea," Alex says. "Slide out this way with me so nobody notices us."

He pulls a wool stadium blanket from the small space behind his seat and climbs out.

I slide across the front seat toward his door, about to tell him he's crazy if he thinks I'm snuggling under a blanket with him.

But he spreads it out in the bed of the truck. "Get up here," he whispers, even though the music from someone else's car stereo drowns him out. Everyone out in the clearing is too busy having fun to notice us.

He doesn't hold his hand out to me again, and for half of a heartbeat, I'm disappointed. I put my hands on the tailgate as he jumps down, and suddenly his hands are on my waist, lifting me up.

I feel dizzy for just a moment. And then he's letting me go and climbing back up after me.

He closes the tailgate and sits down on the blanket. "Now, look up. You can lie down flat here and see the stars."

I do as he tells me and take a deep breath. Alex is right. The clouds from earlier today are gone. The stars out here, even with the bonfire's light, are breathtaking. He lies down beside me, with more than a foot's space between us.

"*I strain my heart, I stretch my hands. And catch at hope,*" he whispers.

That dizzy feeling comes back. The stars are beginning to reel overhead. I close my eyes. His blanket smells like sunshine, like my sheets at home. His moms must use the same laundry detergent as mine does.

"When did you find out?" I ask, not daring to open my eyes. I don't want to see his face yet.

"Yesterday. Before that, I was oblivious. What about you?"

"Walt Whitman."

I don't know what else to say. And he's quiet for a long time too. Is he glad it's me? Was he hoping it was someone else? Or did he just like the idea of writing to someone anonymously?

"What constellation is that directly above us?" Alex asks finally.

When I open my eyes again, I see Leo. The moon hasn't risen yet, and I can see the swath of the Milky Way stretched across the sky. When I tell Alex the name of the constellation, he growls softly, more like a sick lawnmower than a lion. I smile in the darkness, but don't laugh for fear he'll think I want to be friends. Or something.

I point out the brightest stars in the sky to him: Regulus, Arcturus, Castor and Pollux. We see Mars and Jupiter, and I think I see a falling star, but it flits across the sky and disappears before I know for sure if I really saw it or imagined it.

I make a wish anyway. Just to be safe.

We are both silent when we hear Trista and Hank approach the truck. "He's not in the truck—was he with Caleb?" Hank is asking.

I can see Alex's face in the firelight. His cheek is smooth, stubble-free. He's putting his finger on his lips. Fascinated by the shape of his mouth, I can do nothing but nod. I have no desire to join the others just yet either.

"No, Caleb is over in the Dark Corner with Erin," Trista's saying. "Maybe he's with Scott and Dylan."

I watch Alex's face for any signs that the news about Erin bothers him. And why is Alex hiding out with me if Erin's here tonight?

"I'm sorry," I mouth, and he looks at me, puzzled. I don't know if he can't read lips or if he doesn't know why I'm sorry. "Erin," I whisper.

He rolls closer to me, so he can whisper "What about her?" in my ear. His breath is warm and tingly on my cheek. I feel more claustrophobic now than I did inside the truck.

"PLUTO!!!!" Hank yells across the cemetery.

"Come on," Trista is saying. "Let's go see if he's out behind Dylan's van. That's where the real party is."

Alex's stare is intense. I hold his gaze, and I'm ready to apologize for assuming he was here to get high with Dylan and the others. I realize how hard it is for him tonight. I'm glad he's here, hiding out with me instead.

When we hear Trista's shriek and Hank's laughter from the other side of the bonfire, we both take a deep breath. "Now, what about Erin?" Alex asks.

"You two aren't dating?" I feel stupid and hope he doesn't think I am purposely paying attention to his love life. "Natalie and Trista thought so when we saw you together this morning."

Alex rolls his eyes. God, I hope he can't see my blushing cheeks in the dim light. "I was giving her Caleb's history notes. I'd borrowed them from Caleb the day before and she was going to see him before I did." His face grows serious. "Why would you assume I'm hooking up with someone else?"

And here is the discussion I've been dying to have, but I also don't really want to know.

"Iris never talked to me about you," I say, playing with my bracelet nervously. "So I never really knew how serious you two were." I'm admitting to Alex that my twin and I were not as close as twins are expected to be. She kept her secrets. I always wondered if it was because she thought I'd tattle to Mom. But I wouldn't have. It hurts that she didn't trust me, because I told her all of my secrets. She laughed at my angsty crushes and hugged me when I thought the world was conspiring against me.

"Anyway, I didn't mean to be nosy." And I find myself unable to ask the question, *Are you over Iris?* Unwilling to hear his answer.

Before he can say anything, I push up from the blanket in the truck bed and start to climb out. "I need to go," I say. But he grabs my arm, and I topple over, on top of him.

I panic. "Let go!" I whisper, struggling to get away from him.

"Andria," he whispers, as his hands settle on my hips. Part of me wants to quit fighting and lean in closer. The other part of me wants to run.

I'm trapped, and I push up on my hands, trying desperately to stay above him.

His grasp tightens as he squeezes my waist. Nerve endings

all over my body explode like fireworks, and suddenly I feel out of control. It feels wild. Intoxicating.

Oh God, what if I completely lose control? The fear of having a seizure right here and now is very real. My heart is pounding, both from teen monkey lust and sheer terror.

He rolls, and suddenly I'm underneath him, his blue eyes staring at me with an intense, haunted gaze. He must see the fear in my eyes, because he begins to pull away. I put a hand up against his chest, then slowly, I move my fingertips to his mouth.

Alex closes his eyes and rolls back off me and sits up. "I'm sorry," he whispers. "I shouldn't have . . ."

I scramble away from him, suddenly chilled from his body's absence. My heart is still pounding, so hard I'm afraid he can hear it.

He's still staring at me, sad and confused. "I didn't mean . . ." He rubs his face with his hands. "Shit."

This is not my eloquent desk poet talking right now. This is not Alex Hammond, cool rock god of Athens High. This is a boy who needs a friend. "It's okay," I tell him, sitting back with my legs folded under me. "Blame it on the stars. Regulus is a bad influence."

He laughs, even though I know he's not really sure what I'm talking about. I'm babbling. But the intense, haunted look on his face is gone, and before he can say anything else, Hank spots us and yells across the parking lot. "Pluto! Where have you been?"

Dammit.

Alex frowns at me. "Busted."

This makes me smile. "Busted for being the only sober ones here?"

"Something like that."

Hank is pulling a drunk Trista by the hand. She has a black

jacket over that sleeveless top she insisted on wearing tonight. "Dude," Hank slurs. His eyes are red. "What are you doing in the back of your truck?"

"Stargazing."

Hank blinks at Alex, and thankfully doesn't even notice me. He looks up at the sky and squints. "Cool."

Trista, however, does see me in the truck bed with Alex. And she is about to say something when Natalie skips over, with Thomas following her. "What are we doing?" she says. "Is it time to go home? I'm freezing!"

Thomas rolls his eyes. "I thought y'all had a gig tonight in town."

Hank shakes his head. "That's tomorrow."

Natalie blinks, her eyes glassy. "Oh no! What are we going to tell our parents when we want to go see you? My mom thinks we're at the Indigo right now watching you guys play. She won't believe me if I tell her I want to see you play again tomorrow."

"Why not?" Caleb says, joining us. "Calcifer's groupies are very devoted."

Erin giggles as she stumbles up behind him and throws her arms around his waist. "Extremely devoted," she slurs. "Obsessive, even."

Natalie is shivering still. Caleb disentangles himself from Erin in order to take off his jacket and give it to Nat. She blushes as she puts it on. "Thanks," she whispers.

"Anything for a fan," he says, smiling to her.

"Hey," Erin pouts.

"What I want to know is," Trista says, "why in the hell are Andria and Alex hooking up in the back of his truck?"

All six pairs of drunken eyes turn toward us.

"Oh, for God's sake," Alex mumbles.

Natalie reaches for my hand and tries to pull me out of the

truck. I climb out on my own, and Alex jumps down from the back.

"Get away from him," she says. "You need to come home with us so we can talk about him and all these other lovely boys." She glances from Thomas to Caleb.

Alex's face is clouded with worry, but he makes no move to hold on to me. "Wait, no one is in any condition to drive right now except me."

"And Andria," Trista says. "Oh no, that's right. She can't drive either." She pouts and hangs on to Hank. They are barely able to hold each other upright.

I'm trying to figure out if she's being malicious or just stupid as Alex runs his fingers through his short hair in exasperation. "All right," he says. "Trista, where is Selena?"

Trista shrugs as she glances around the park. "Jack was supposed to meet her when he got off work. But I don't see his car either."

"Perfect," he says with a sigh. "All right. I can take two people in the front and smuggle the rest of you in the back. But God help us if we get stopped."

"Woot!" Hank jumps up into the bed of the truck, with Caleb, Erin, and Thomas trying to climb up after him. Thomas grabs the blanket and covers up the giggling pile of drunk teenagers.

"I want to be inside where there's heat," Natalie says, opening the passenger door.

Trista hops in right after her. "Me too. Fuck riding out there."

Alex grabs my arm, gently pulling me with him. "Get in on my side. We'll make room."

I'm not thrilled at the thought of practically sitting in Alex's lap, but it's a much better option than riding in the back with the drunken horde and freezing to death.

"Turn the heater on!" Trista and Natalie scream as I get in.

Alex gets in right after me and starts up the engine. I scoot over as far as I can without sitting on top of Natalie, but my thigh is still pressed up against Alex's. My skin is on fire long before the heater kicks in and thaws out my friends.

Alex looks straight ahead and is silent as he drives back into town, stopping first at Caleb's house. Hank pokes his head out from the blanket to yell a "Woot!" at Caleb before Thomas smacks him upside the head.

Erin's house is next, in the same neighborhood.

Thomas and Hank get out together at Thomas's house, which is the same fancy riverfront neighborhood where Natalie lives. Trista rolls down her window so Hank can lean in and kiss her good-night. "Call me," he says.

His beer breath has now infected the whole inside of the truck. Alex rolls down his own window.

"Jesus!" Trista says, rolling hers up. "We're going to die of pneumonia."

"Fresh air is good for you," Alex says as he pulls out of Thomas's driveway. He puts his arm across the top of the seat, and the hairs on the back of my neck come alive.

I wonder what he would do if I laid my head against his arm. If anyone else would notice.

When we pull up in front of the Romans' home, Trista opens her door. "Oops," she says, tripping as Natalie pushes her out of the way. They both fall onto the dew-filled grass and burst out laughing.

I don't look up at Alex. I don't know what happened between us tonight, but it feels . . . weird. And scary. And maybe a little . . . nice?

"See you Monday," he says.

"Be careful," is all I can think to say. At least all the drunks are dropped off someplace safe. I hope Natalie's parents don't wake up with all the noise these two are making.

"You too."

I shut the passenger door and wonder what he thinks I have to be careful about. The only thing I'm in danger of right now is falling in love with the wrong boy.

CHAPTER 16

Seven Days

It's after eleven on Saturday morning, and I'm the first one awake. I sneak downstairs to the kitchen to find something to take my pills with. I have this morning's doses in a blue old-lady pill container.

Natalie's mom is frosting cupcakes. It smells like coconut and cherries and something else. "The first creature emerges from the lair!" she says. "Coffee?" she asks, nodding toward their Keurig. "Mugs are in the cabinet above."

I smile. I love Natalie's mom. "What kind of cupcakes are you making?" I ask as I poke through her basket of K-cups. I pick out a mocha.

"Amaretto. These are for a friend's baby shower this afternoon. But there are chocolate donuts in the oven for you girls."

"Smells heavenly." I'm dumping my third spoonful of sugar into my mug when Natalie drags herself into the kitchen and plops herself on a barstool.

She puts her head down on the bar. "I need sugar." Her voice is muffled by her crossed arms. "I'm dying of low blood sugar."

I grin at Mrs. Roman as she pulls the donuts out of the oven. She arranges them on a pretty china plate and sets it on the bar. "Voilà. Sugar."

"It's like magic!" Natalie says, lifting her head back up. "Thank you, Mommy."

Mrs. Roman rolls her eyes. "Okay, girls. Don't make your-selves sick. I have to get these cupcakes over to Bethany's house. Andria, is your mom picking you up or do you need a ride home?"

Not having a license sucks. "My stepdad can get me. Mom's got an open house in Dogwood Trace."

Mrs. Roman nods as she finishes packing up her cupcakes. "Pretty houses out there. See you girls later."

As soon as her mom leaves, Natalie puts her donut down. "So, was I imagining things or were you hanging out with Alex Hammond last night?"

"We were the only two sober people there."

"So you weren't, like, hooking up?" I can't tell for sure, but it looks like there's a glimmer of hope in her eyes. Or possibly worry.

"Are you kidding me? Why would I be interested in him? And why the hell would he be interested in me?"

She shrugs with a sad smile. "I guess it would be weird, right?"

"What would be weird?" Trista says, yawning in the doorway. "Ooh, caffeine." She rummages through the basket of coffee.

"If Andria and Alex started going out."

Trista lets the Extra Bold Mountain Blend cup fall out of her hand as she stares at me. "Beyond weird. Alternate-universe weird. Andria, are you alternate-universe Andria? Have you come in peace?"

I roll my eyes. "Don't worry. All is still right with this universe. Alex and I are not going out." I glance at Natalie as I grab a donut. "And we never will."

She sighs. "I still think he's a little unstable. But you would look cute together."

Trista goes back to brewing her coffee. "Because he looked cute with her twin sister. That's messed up, Nat. Besides, didn't we see him with Erin yesterday?"

Natalie licks chocolate glaze off her fingers. God, why can't my mom make homemade donuts instead of quinoa and flaxseed muffins? "But then Erin was with Caleb last night."

"Anyway, I think you were right when you said Alex was still not over Iris," I say. "And I'm not into drug addicts."

Trista hmmphs as she brings her mug of coffee to the bar and grabs a donut. "Even if he's not an addict anymore, and even if he wasn't still hung up on Iris, you can do much better. Pluto Alex has a billion issues. And I don't think you can fix that."

Natalie shrugs. "Well, he is a . . . complicated person."

I huddle over my coffee and frown. "What I want to know is, why are you with Thomas when Caleb is your knight in shining armor? You wore his jacket home last night."

Natalie blushes. "He chose to hang out with Erin. And Thomas would have given me his jacket if I'd asked him."

"But you didn't have to ask Caleb," I point out, taking my pills out of my baggie. I line them up on the counter. Pink circle, blue oval, pink oval. My coffee is cool enough to swallow the pills without burning my throat.

I hate taking medicine in front of my friends. It reminds them that I'm not like them. And so very different from Iris.

"Seven days!!!" Natalie squeals.

"Are we still going to Six Flags?" Trista asks.

"Ugh. Not with me driving." My stomach is starting to hurt again. I grab another donut.

But Trista doesn't argue. "Selena can take us," she says. "If we don't mind paying for her ticket and for gas."

"We have to pay for Andria's ticket too," Natalie says. "It's her celebration."

"No, I'm happy to pay. If my mom lets me go. She thinks rides can cause seizures."

"So we don't tell her where we're going and we buy your ticket."

Trista sips her coffee in silence. She probably thinks I'm afraid of having a seizure. And she's right. Losing control in front of my friends is one of my biggest fears.

"I'd better call Craig," I say, sliding down from the barstool. "Tell your mom the donuts were wonderful."

"Aw, don't leave yet," Natalie says. "We could go get lunch."

"At the Indigo?" Trista's face lights up with a malicious grin.

I scream at them in frustration as I make my way back up the stairs to find my phone.

My stepdad picks me up within the hour, with the roof down on his Mercedes. He has been golfing with potential investors in his new subdivision west of the Perimeter. He's been begging Mom to let us move out there, and promises her the house of her dreams. It's in a better school district too, but Mom loves our historic neighborhood. I don't think he can talk her into moving.

"How was your pajama party? Lots of pillow fights and girl talk?"

Dork. "Yep," I mutter, throwing my bags in his backseat.

"Are you hungry? Want to get some lunch?"

"No, thank you."

"I get it, you've probably been eating all sorts of yummy

stuff made by Mrs. Roman." He grins. "Don't worry, I won't tell."

"Ha-ha. I don't know what you're talking about."

His cell phone rings, and when he sees the number on the display, he sets the call to private instead of answering on his steering wheel. "Business," he whispers to me. "Hello, this is Craig Williams." It's silly, though. With the top down, it's not like he could hear on speaker anyway.

I push my hair out of my face and try not to eavesdrop as we drive down Broad Street. Someone is walking out of the Lutheran church. Alex.

"Yes . . . yes," Craig is saying. "Of course."

Alex looks up just as we pass by, and he recognizes me. Instead of smiling or giving a friendly wave, he frowns.

"No, I'm afraid that's not possible right now," Craig says. He turns off Broad, and I stare straight ahead. What is Alex's problem?

I try to remember if I said anything last night to piss him off. Maybe he didn't recognize me, but I'm almost certain he did.

"Let me get back to you on this," Craig is saying. "I'm in the middle of something at the moment. . . . Of course. We'll talk soon."

As he pulls into the driveway, he sighs. "I guess I'm going to have to go back into the office for a bit. Tell your mom I'll be home before supper."

"Sure. Thanks for the ride." I get my stuff from the backseat and dig my house key out of my purse.

He waits until I get the front door unlocked before waving and backing out. Mom's open house isn't over until five. She has left me a note on the kitchen counter: *Did you remember to take your pills???*

I toss the note in the trash and head back to my room. My phone has a few missed texts when I plug it in the charger. From Natalie: *I really do miss Caleb.* ☹

And from Trista: *Nat really should be with Caleb. Let's go beat up Erin.* ☺

I smile. Natalie must have opened up to Trista after I left. I'm glad I agreed to hang out with them last night, but there is still a huge distance between me and them. And I don't know if that's a bad thing. I never was a part of the soccer team so I never was as close to all of the girls as Iris. I didn't go on the out-of-town trips for play-off games or tournaments. Rarely got to hang out with them at Pizza Hut after games or practices. Nat and I will always be friends, but never as close as Iris and Tris were. And if Nat and Tris become closer friends now, I'm okay with that.

And really, Caleb can be a nice guy. But I'm not sure if Natalie would be better off with him or Thomas. Or maybe neither.

The coffee I drank at the Romans' this morning is fading fast, and since I have nothing better to do, I lie down to take a nap.

It's not restful, though. I keep waking up, sometimes because the room is too hot, and sometimes because I've kicked the covers off and am freezing. I swear my phone vibrates, but every time I lift my head to check it, there's no new message.

I dream of Iris. At Rock 'n' Roll Graveyard. She's looking up at the stars and telling me I'm missing the best part. I tell her I know.

Mom wakes me when she comes home. My room is dark, and she fusses at me for sleeping all day. My head hurts.

I sit up and yawn. It's not like I really got any rest. Iris was telling me to look for the Pleiades.

"Did you have a good time with the girls?" Mom asks. She's going through the mail as she sits on the side of my bed. "Mrs. Roman said everyone was excited about going to see the band play last night."

"I had fun. Thanks for talking me into going."

She pats my knee under the quilt. "Dinner will be ready in about an hour. Want to come help me with the vegetables?"

The doorbell rings, and she tells me she'll meet me in the kitchen. But when I get out front, she's standing at the door, talking to a police officer. My stomach twists violently. It's about last night. I know I wasn't drinking, but I'm sure there's some other sort of law I was breaking. Trespassing?

"I don't understand. How can I help you?" Mom's voice is pleasant. The same one she uses when little girls come to the door to sell cookie dough.

The police officer is a tiny young man. He looks uncomfortable on our front porch step. A larger, older female cop stands behind him, her hand on her gun belt. She looks at Mom menacingly. "Mrs. Williams, I'm sorry, but we have a warrant to search your husband's office. We need to take his computer."

"What do you think he's done?" Mom's voice is eerily calm. Like nothing is wrong. But the police are here because they think my stepfather is some sort of criminal.

"We received a phone call from a concerned parent that Mr. Williams may be engaging in inappropriate activity with one of the girls on his soccer team. Do you know when Mr. Williams will be home?"

"What sort of inappropriate activity?" Mom asks. "He said he had some work to do at the office . . . but he should be home anytime now."

"Please, ma'am. We need to have access to his computer." The young cop holds up a piece of paper. An official-looking paper.

"Mom," I say, tugging on her arm. I don't think she wants to move. But she needs to let them do their job before she gets into trouble.

When she looks at me, her eyes are glassy. I don't know

what the hell Craig has done, but he should burn in hell if he has hurt Mom, after everything else she's gone through. "Let them do their job, Mom."

She lets me lead her out of the way, and the two cops invade our house. Even the short one seems larger than life in our living room. The room spins a little, and I realize Mom is seeing the same thing I am: the night six months ago when the cops stood in the living room while the EMTs carried Iris's body out the door.

I squeeze Mom's hand. This is not the same, I remind myself.

"Can you tell me exactly what my husband is accused of?" Mom asks.

But the female cop is looking at me. "Sweetie, I need to speak with you for a moment about your stepfather. Alone."

"Why?" Mom clutches my hand now. "She hasn't done anything wrong."

"Of course not, Mrs. Williams. But we need to ask her a few questions about her relationship with Mr. Williams."

"Relationship?" I let go of Mom's hand. "Do you mean what I think you mean? Gross. He's a normal stepdad. I can tell you that right here."

"He picked you up from your friend's house this morning and brought you home, right?"

"Have you been following him?" Mom asks. Craig must be in serious trouble if this investigation has been going on for a while.

"Yes."

"Andria, has Craig ever been inappropriate with you or anyone else that you've witnessed? You don't have to talk about this in front of your mom if it's uncomfortable."

"Ew. No." Nothing I've ever noticed. "Are you saying he's molesting girls on the soccer team?" I think of Natalie and Trista and can't imagine it. Trista would never let something happen to her without fighting back. She'd kick Craig's ass. Unless—ew.

"Or is someone sleeping with him?" I ask before thinking. Mom gasps.

The younger policeman comes out of the den with Craig's desktop. He glances at his partner.

She hands Mom a business card with a phone number and a badge number written on it. "Mr. Williams needs to speak with us. It would be better if he cooperates and comes in willingly."

But as they open the front door to leave, Craig pulls up in his convertible. I move to follow the cops outside, but Mom grabs my arm. Hard. "Don't. The neighbors will see you."

Mr. Nosy Old Guy is probably already camped out on his porch, looking at the cop car. The neighbors will know what happens whether we attempt to hide it or not. I try not to think about school on Monday. I still don't know what is happening. Whose parents are accusing Craig?

The female cop pokes her head back inside. "Mr. Williams has agreed to come with us to the police station willingly."

Craig is standing on the porch with them. "I'm sorry, Patrice." He doesn't look at either of us, but turns and follows the police to their car. They don't handcuff him, but he slides into the backseat, where bad people go. Is he a bad person?

What does "I'm sorry" mean? I close the front door and turn around to find Mom sinking down onto the floor, sobbing.

"Andria, baby. Did he touch you? I swear to Christ I will kill him myself."

"What? No!" I put my arms around her. "Maybe this is a mistake. Maybe he made one of the players mad and she's just trying to cause him trouble."

Mom shakes her head. "What if it's not a mistake? That bastard! He's been . . . different lately. Distant. Working late. Extra out of-town trips." She wipes her face, with a bitter laugh. "And here I was worried he was sleeping with his secretary."

A million different things are flying through my head right now. I don't know what to do. What to say to Mom. How are we going to get through this? If Craig was sleeping with one of the girls on the team, Mom will be devastated. The cops were so worried about him doing something with me. A nasty thought slithers up from deep inside my brain. It stops my blood cold.

What if he was doing something with Iris?

CHAPTER 17

Six Days

I can't remember the last time I had a decent night's sleep. I toss and turn, my worries tumbling over and over inside my head. Mostly I worry about my mother. How much more sadness can she handle?

Sophie whimpers and tries to climb up on my bed. She knows better, but this morning I let her snuggle with me. I need her right now.

It's not even five in the morning, and I hear Mom rummaging in Iris's room. She can't sleep either. She's looking for my sister's diary. Mom looked six months ago but never found it. It was navy blue with a silver unicorn on the cover. She'd had it since she was thirteen.

I know I'm not going to sleep anymore, so I get up and go to help Mom look.

"Do you have any idea where she hid it?" she asks. She looks like she's been crying, but she's not crying now. She's calm. Determined. On a mission.

"Did you look under her mattress?"

"Of course. That's the first place I looked six months ago. And the closet shelves, and in her dresser drawers."

"Look again. The last time I ever saw her write in it, she was lying in bed."

"Help me, then." Together we throw the pillows off the bed and tug the mattress over. There's a folded-up poster board from an elementary school project. The science fair project she won a blue ribbon for in sixth grade. I helped her make an astrolabe.

I lift up the poster board and find her diary. Mom is shaking. Either with anger or fear, or a little of both. "You knew it was here?"

I shake my head. I've always had a pretty good idea where it might be, but I never went searching for it.

"And you never told me."

"Honestly, I hadn't thought about it. I haven't seen her write in it in years." For the longest time, we knew everything about one another. It never occurred to me that she had any secrets. Because I didn't.

I live a boring life. Other than the time I tried to steal Craig's motorcycle. Or drink Mom's brandy. For that, Iris yelled at me for days. She knew alcohol and my meds didn't mix. She took the brandy away and finished it herself.

"What if there was something in here about Craig?" Mom asks.

A sick feeling grows in my stomach. She is right. Whatever secrets Iris kept in this diary might have saved someone else a lot of pain. She picks up the diary.

"I don't want to read this," she says. "This is probably just full of in-depth descriptions of her dates."

Alex is probably in there, I think, staring at the unicorn on the cover. I don't want to read it either. "We could read it together," I say. Even though I dread it as much as she does.

We let the mattress fall back down and both sit on the side of the bed. "Ready?" Mom asks as she opens the book.

I scoot closer to her and crane my neck to see.

It's more awful than I imagined. Craig began touching Iris when we were twelve. Right after Mom gave us our own bedrooms. She wonders early on if he visits my room too, and at first is relieved when he tells her I'm too sickly for him. Later, she gets paranoid and decides she has to be jealous of me. One day it's because I'm not the one being abused. The next day it's because she fears she will have to share Craig with me.

I can't believe the way that monster warped her mind. I want to throw up as I read.

Mom gasps as she sees the same words I see on the page. "But she had boyfriends. She'd been dating since ninth grade," she says. She's trying to convince herself that what we're reading isn't true.

"And he fought you on that, remember?" I say. "Craig thought we were both too young to date." Not that anyone ever asked me out. But Craig never liked Noah, Iris's first boyfriend. And he certainly didn't like Alex.

Mom begins to flip through the pages. Iris and Craig's relationship (ick, I hate to use that word) became something more consensual as the years went by. Even though she still knew it was wrong. She thought that he loved her. And she wrote last Christmas that she loved him. "Who was the boy she dated before Alex? The one with the El Camino?"

"Mike?" Mike was a drug dealer. I know this now, but didn't the first time I met him. Now I'm not even sure if his name really is Mike. She was dating him last summer, but it's evident from the diary that she was just using him to get drugs. By this time, she was depressed and believed she needed to make Craig leave her alone, but he wouldn't.

My stomach feels queasy as I think about the last time I saw Mike. The night Iris died. She'd taken me with her to his party somewhere on the other side of the university. Out near the edge of town. I had had a seizure earlier that evening and had made her promise not to tell anyone. In exchange for her silence, I had to go with her and drive her home in case she got too drunk.

She was more than happy to keep my secret about the seizure, because she knew I'd be obligated to keep that night's party a secret too. I had trapped myself. And her. And in the end, it didn't help me at all.

Iris has filled these pages with her pain. The things she couldn't tell me, she poured out into this book. My cheeks are wet with my tears as I read page after page. How could we have not known this was going on?

Mom throws the book down and runs to the bathroom between our bedrooms. I can hear her being violently ill.

I pick up the diary, so full of poison and suffering. I flip through the pages, searching for her last entry. There's no date, but it must have been written sometime within the last week or two that she was alive.

Not sure what Alex thinks or feels anymore, but I don't think we're meant to be together. He's too intense for me, too much for me to handle right now. I think he knows it, too.

I don't know if he really knew it or not. I guess I know now how she felt about him, but how did Alex feel about her?

Mom is reluctant to let me go to school. She thinks my classmates are going to harass me. Or ask me stupid questions. Or at the very least, stare at me with pity.

That isn't anything new. Kids have stared at me since the day I had a seizure in kindergarten. "I want to make sure Natalie and Trista are okay," I tell her. Mom's face pales when she realizes how many of my classmates might be affected by this.

I wear my favorite hoodie, favorite jeans, and black boots. I'm dressed for battle.

She is not going in to work today, so she drops me off at school. "I love you," she says as I open the car door. She looks small this morning. Frail and terribly human.

"Love you too," I say as I face the crowd in front of the main building. What doesn't kill me makes me stronger. I ignore that twisty feeling I'm getting in my stomach. Make it to the library, I tell myself. I can hide out in there until the bell rings.

No one stares at me in the hallway. Perhaps the news hasn't gotten out yet. I sneak into the library just as Verla is unlocking the doors.

"Hey, how are you and your mom holding up?" she asks, her eyes sad.

The news is out there after all.

"When did you hear?" I ask.

"It was in the paper this morning online. Andria, I'm surprised your mother let you come to school today."

Ugh. It won't be long before everyone knows. "I'll be fine."

Verla plays with the silver necklace around her neck. "My door is always open, honey. If you ever need to talk, you know I'm here. I'll even share my chocolate."

"I guess the paper didn't say the name of the student accusing Craig."

"No, they won't be allowed to, since she's a minor."

But gossip gets around the school quickly, and by the time we're seated in first block, Natalie knows. She reaches over and squeezes my hand. "Kimber isn't here today. They're saying her family took her out of school and sent her to stay with her cousins in Florida."

Kimber is gorgeous. And extremely talented on the soccer

field. I hope she is strong enough to survive this. "I wish I'd known."

"How could you have?" Natalie says, shocked. "None of us ever suspected this. Craig was the best soccer coach ever. Do you think maybe he just went a little crazy after Iris's death?"

"She probably went after him," Trista says. "That's what Thomas is saying." Thomas dated Kimber briefly last year. But she dumped him when she found out he was messing around with two cheerleaders.

"No, Craig is the adult and he is the one to blame." They both look taken aback by my sudden fierceness. I don't know if Iris's story will have to come out, but if it will help Kimber, then I know Mom is willing to turn in the diary. Until then, I promised her I wouldn't tell anyone about Iris and Craig.

By lunchtime, more people are beginning to talk and stare, so Natalie and Trista keep me company in the library. Verla ignores us as we eat fruit snacks from the vending machine in the periodical section.

In English, we are finishing up our Antigone unit. Mr. Dawkins wants an essay arguing either Creon's view or Antigone's view about her brother's death and burial. He's giving us the period to write, but I don't want to think about ancient Greek soap-opera drama right now. I have enough drama in present-day Athens, thank you very much.

I write poetry instead, lines that I copied from the desk in algebra. Lines from a Gary Snyder poem that Alex must have left for me.

I love the simple rhythm of the words, the smoky imagery of the Pleiades. I wonder if Alex was out running again last night. And then I wonder if he ran past my house. I think of Iris's diary entry. "He's too much for me to handle right now." If he was too much then, what is he now?

He's not in the library after school. I don't know what he

thinks about Craig's arrest, or if he even cares. Verla hauls the last tote of poetry books up to my table.

"You guys have done a really fantastic job cataloging these books for me," she says. "The school has decided to hold a poetry fair in here since April is Poetry Month. Sort of like a reading fair but the displays have to be about poets."

"Sounds awesome," I tell her. "Will the projects be for a grade or will they be extra credit?"

She shrugs. "I'm waiting to hear back from the English department on that. Of all of these poets, have you found a favorite?"

There are too many, I think, looking at the stacks of books we've already cataloged. I still love Sylvia Plath, but now I'm also fond of Robert Frost and Emily Dickinson.

I shrug.

Verla grins. "I know, it's like trying to pick your favorite child." But I don't have kids, and I'm pretty sure she doesn't either. "Have some chocolate before you get started. Just don't get fingerprints on the books."

She doesn't mention the missing Alex Hammond, and I don't ask.

CHAPTER 18

The girls are still at practice as I leave the library. One of the PE teachers, Mrs. Coulson, is standing at the side of the field, whistle in her mouth. I'm glad Tris and Nat and the others don't have to give up soccer because of Craig. Tris has been excited about the upcoming championship games in Macon.

Mom was waiting until evening to sneak into her office so she could get work done without a crowd, so I'm not in a hurry to go home. She's probably been moping or making some paleo/gluten-free/bean concoction for comfort food. To me, comfort food is fried dill pickles. I hope I can talk the girls into going to the Indigo with me.

I'm not going because I want to see Alex. I swear it's because of the pickles. And they have the best crushed ice in the drink machine. I love Diet Coke with crushed pellet ice.

Mrs. Coulson calls the girls over to the sidelines and gathers them in a huddle. I can't hear what she's saying, but I see Trista's stormy face. She catches my eye but doesn't smile.

They're talking about Craig. Waiting for them is probably a bad idea.

The huddle of girls breaks up, and Natalie runs over to me. "Hey, you doing all right?"

I nod. "I just wondered if y'all want to go get food with me. We could walk over to the Indigo Dragon. My treat."

She grins. "I'm so hungry I don't even want to stop for a shower. Let me grab Trista."

Trista is starving too. The rest of the team heads for the locker room, but we start walking toward Main Street. Indigo is only a short fifteen-minute walk from the school.

"Ugh, do you have deodorant in your purse?" Trista asks Natalie as she sniffs her shirt. It's only slightly damp.

She pulls out a stick, and they share it.

Ick. "Are you sure y'all don't want to shower first?"

Trista laughs. "Don't want to get my hair wet. Besides, those chicken poppers that Alex's mom makes are the bomb of the mother-effing bay."

Natalie rolls her eyes but grins. She stuffs the deodorant back into her bag. "I wonder what the soup of the day is."

"Whatever," Trista says. "It's too hot for soup."

But the chill on her moist skin is enough to make her change her mind when we get to the Indigo. "Oooh, I need a big bowl of black bean soup."

The place is quiet this time of day. Alex isn't out front. One of his moms is working the counter. I tell myself it is not disappointment I feel creeping outward from the center of my chest. I still get to eat fried dill pickles. There's no reason in the world why I should feel disappointed.

And the ice. Can't forget about the awesome ice they have here.

We give Mrs. Hammond our orders, and I pay with my debit card. Mom says to only use it in emergencies and she monitors my account, but I think today qualifies as a Category 5 shit storm. A basket of fried dill pickles with Cajun ranch dipping sauce and a giant Diet Coke. I add two orders of banana pudding to share at home with Mom. She needs real comfort food too.

As we sit down in a booth by the window, Tris and Nat across from me, a few more girls from the soccer team walk in. Erin, freshly showered and looking perfect, waves as she and the others go up to the counter to order.

Natalie frowns and is suddenly very interested in her chili cheese fries.

"What's wrong?" I ask. I need to hear some normal high school drama. Anything to take my mind off my own family's disaster.

"Caleb," Trista mutters, stealing one of Nat's fries. She is still waiting for her burger to come out.

I glance back at Erin and the other girls at the counter. A few of them are glaring at us and whispering. "Is he still seeing her?" I ask.

Nat's face is suddenly pale, her eyes a little too bright.

"What did he do?" I ask Trista.

She shrugs as Erin and Melissa walk over to our booth. "It's such a shame about Mr. Craig," Melissa says.

"Do you think Kimber is going to get in trouble?" Erin asks. "I mean, she practically threw herself at him after last week's game."

"What evidence do they have?" Natalie asks me. The entire girls' varsity soccer team stares at me expectantly.

I shrug. "The cops said a parent had filed a complaint. And they came and took Craig's computer."

"What was on his computer?" Erin asks, wide-eyed.

"No clue."

"Seriously?" Melissa's glare does not intimidate me. Instead it pisses me off.

"Seriously. I have no idea if there's Candy Crush or child pornography on his computer. I have no idea what my stepdad does in his spare time. Besides coach girls' soccer and watch old James Bond movies."

Everyone is silent. I feel the wall between me and them growing thicker. I never was a part of their group. And now with Iris gone and—with any luck—the soccer coach of the year gone, I never will be.

Which doesn't bother me. Not too much.

I try to slide out of the booth, poking Trista. "Let me out," I whisper.

But she doesn't. "Y'all need to back the fuck off. Whether Craig is guilty or not, it's not Andria's fault. We all worshipped Craig. Can you imagine how hard this must be for her? For her mom?"

The tense dramatic moment is destroyed by Alex sliding a plate with an enormous hamburger and french fries across the table toward us. He doesn't look at me, but glances at Trista instead. "The banana pudding will be here shortly."

"Thanks. Can you bring me some ketchup?" she calls. He's already halfway back to the kitchen.

Without another word, he disappears in the kitchen then comes back out with a bottle of Heinz. This time, he does look at me. But his eyes look sad. Full of pity.

Trista nudges me. "You haven't even touched your pickles. Pickles are supposed to make everything better." She steals one and dunks it in my Cajun ranch dressing.

"Tell your mom we're thinking about her," Erin says, as she and Melissa take their to-go orders and head out.

Natalie is frowning, lost in thought.

"Hey," I say, leaning over. "What is going on?"

"Caleb called me last night, apologizing for the way he's been acting. I thought he wanted to get back together. He said he was just hanging out with Erin because I told him I didn't want to see him. But I don't know if Erin really likes him or not. I don't want to lose her friendship over him. I don't know if he's really worth it, you know?"

My heart hurts for Natalie. She deserves someone who worships the ground she walks on. "Does she know about Caleb's history with you?"

Nat shrugs. "If she knows that he called me last night, she certainly doesn't act like it's bothering her."

"Should we tell her?" I ask. "If he's stringing both of you along, he needs an ass-kicking."

Trista snorts. But before we can plot any kicking of Caleb's ass, the door opens and the devil himself walks in, accompanied by his shadow.

"PLUTO!" Caleb shouts across the café. Hank is slinking in behind him, both boys looking particularly moody.

Alex pokes his head out from the kitchen. "Find a seat, guys. I'll be right there."

Trista waves them over to our booth. Of course. Caleb sees Nat and brightens up. He tries to sit down next to her, but she slides away from him.

"I've been trying to call you," he says, oblivious to the wrath he has incurred.

Trista and Hank are oblivious to everything but each other's tongues.

"Ready to leave?" I ask Nat.

"But we just got here," Caleb says, stealing one of Nat's chili cheese fries.

She pulls her plate out of his reach. "You should leave, Caleb."

I stare across the table at her in shock. Natalie is usually quiet in her stubbornness. I've never heard her stand up to a boy before.

Caleb nudges her, just as shocked that she's saying no to him. "Come on, baby. I thought we were past all of that. I said I was sorry."

Trista pulls on Hank, and they move to another booth, leaving me as the lone, awkward witness to this conversation. I think about excusing myself to go to the bathroom, but Natalie looks up at me, her puppy-dog eyes pleading. I stay, and tear the napkin in my lap into tiny shreds.

"What did you tell Erin?" she asks him.

"What are you talking about?" He tries to grab her hand, but she moves it away. "I told you she meant nothing to me."

"But do you know what you mean to her? Did you tell her you wanted to get back together with me?"

He puts one arm across the back of the booth and tries to nuzzle the side of Natalie's neck. "I don't care about her, Natalie."

"She deserves better, Caleb. And I'm beginning to think I deserve better, too." She pushes him out of her way and slides out of the booth. She narrowly misses running into Alex, who's carrying a tray of drinks. With a huff, she storms off to the bathroom.

Caleb looks at me sheepishly and shrugs. "Is it that time of the month?"

"Here," Alex says, setting a root beer down for Caleb. He knows his friends well. "Is Natalie all right?" he asks me.

Caleb leans his arms back and stretches. "Forget about her, man. I need some food."

I roll my eyes and slide out around Alex. "Excuse me."

He takes a step back, but not far enough back for my comfort. I smell Mexican spices and chocolate on him. I want to ask if he's been baking, but I don't want him to think I'm flirting with him. I'm not.

I have to check on Natalie. She needs me right now. I can hear Alex across the café as I push the bathroom door open. "All right, dick. What do you want to eat?" he asks Caleb.

I'm giggling when I push open the bathroom door.

Natalie stands over the sink, glaring at me in the mirror.

"Alex just called Caleb a dick."

She doesn't smile.

"I really do deserve better, don't I?" she asks, her hand on her hip. "Caleb's birthday, I baked him a whole batch of Mom's Death By Chocolate cupcakes and got him tickets to see Mogwai. Know what he did for my birthday?"

I shake my head.

"He spent the whole evening playing video games with my little brother and Hank."

"He didn't take you out?"

"He brought over a bag of Doritos, handed it to me with a 'happy birthday, babe,' and then opened the bag up himself."

"He really is a dick," I say. "When we get to college, we'll find smart, affectionate, polite boys. Maybe even a foreign student with a sexy accent."

Natalie still doesn't smile. "That's over a year away. And there are no good ones left at Athens High."

"I know," I say, sighing as I lean back against the wall. "And none worth fixing up."

She stares at me in the mirror. "Not even Alex?"

I feel my cheeks grow hot. "What do you mean, not even Alex?" I don't know if I could handle Alex moving on with Natalie. They . . . they wouldn't be right for each other.

"You two have been spending an awful lot of time together lately. And it's been six months now. Don't you think it's time he started dating again?"

A knife twists in my chest. A stupid knife that shouldn't even be there. "Do you like him?"

Natalie's eyes grow wide. "Me? God, no, you doofus. I meant you should go out with him!"

"That would be too weird," I say, ignoring the relief I feel in my chest. "And didn't you say he's still not over Iris?"

She shrugs. "Maybe you could be the one to fix him."

"I'm not that handy."

Natalie's eyes grow soft. "Andria, sometimes I think you're broken, too. Iris's death was harder on you than anyone else. What if you can fix each other? What if your demons can fight his demons?"

"What if his demons defeat mine? Then what would happen to me?" Maybe that's what scares me the most. Losing what I have left of Iris. Even if it's only the pain of missing her.

Natalie sighs as she turns back to the mirror and plays with her hair. "Okay, I'm going back out there. I have a psych paper that needs an outline and I brought my notes."

"I'm going to walk home."

"You don't want to call your mom?"

I shake my head. "She wanted to wait until this evening to go in to her office and work, when she wouldn't have to deal with a lot of people. I'll be fine."

"This has got to suck for her." Natalie frowns.

"I think she's in shock. But she's tough. Look how she dealt with Iris's death. She'll be okay." I hope.

"Let me know if I can do anything." She moves to give me a hug, but I turn and push the door open before she can reach me. The last time any of my friends hugged me, it was at Iris's funeral. I'm done reminiscing for the day.

"I'll see you tomorrow," I say over my shoulder and hurry back to our booth to grab my things.

Caleb is gone, and Trista and Hank are sharing a basket of chicken poppers. Hank smiles, and I am astonished when I see the affection in his eyes when he looks at her. When he's sober, he really is in love with Trista. And it makes me happy for her.

I do not search for Alex. I get my book bag and tell Trista and Hank good-bye.

"Is Nat okay?"

"She'll be out in a second," I tell them. "Just keep Caleb away from her and she'll be fine."

Trista gives Hank's hand a quick squeeze and slides out of the booth. "Let me go check on her."

I turn to leave, and my book bag accidentally bumps Alex, who has snuck up behind me with two bowls of soup.

"Watch out!" he says, a split second before black bean soup sloshes all over me. "Dammit, I'm sorry."

I jump back, but the soup is already soaking through the sleeve of my hoodie. I pull it off before I get third-degree burns. The shirt I'm wearing underneath is safe. Mostly. But there's a giant wet spot across my stomach. "I'm sorry," I say. "I'm the one who wasn't paying attention."

He doesn't look injured. "Let me take these back to the kitchen and get you cleaned up. Follow me."

Trista is already dabbing me with paper napkins. Ineffective, but I appreciate her effort.

"Thanks, but I'm fine," I say. Fortunately, I caught most of the soup and there's little spilled on the floor. I grab another napkin and wipe up the drops.

"Come on," Alex says, gently pulling me by the arm. "Into the back with you, where there's a spare T-shirt you can borrow."

I let him lead me through the kitchen all the way to the back of the restaurant, into a tiny cramped office. He closes the door and pulls a T-shirt from the shelf. "Here. It might be a little large, but it should keep you dry until you get home."

He places the T-shirt in my hand and I stare at him, until he finally blushes and turns around.

I hold out the shirt to read the front. It's the same black Indigo Dragon shirt he's wearing. "Does this mean I have to wash dishes to pay for the soup?" I ask.

He starts to turn back around just as I pull my wet shirt off. I'm too stunned to yell at him. And too frightened by the look in his eyes.

I back up against the door, in nothing but a very tight black tank top. Alex takes a step toward me. I'm afraid he's going to kiss me. I'm terrified he won't.

I shiver, and even though I think it's from passion, it's probably because I'm freezing to death. He looks down and frowns, his hands sliding down my arms, and I know he can feel the goose bumps.

I'm losing him. Desperate, I reach for him. I pull his head down to mine so I can kiss him before he can start thinking again. Before he can talk himself out of kissing me.

Before I can talk myself out of kissing him.

It works. His hands slide down to my waist and pull me against him. His lips meet mine gently at first, and then grow bolder, almost hungry. I want my kiss to let him know it's okay. It's all going to be all right. But I don't know how to kiss like that. And even if I did, I don't know if he would understand.

When Alex pulls back, he presses his lips against my forehead. "What are we doing?" he whispers against my skin.

I ignore the sarcastic answer that pops into my head, *Solving polynomial equations, what do you think?* and sigh instead. "I don't know," I whisper finally.

He leans down, and I think he's going to kiss me again, when there is a knock on the door. "Alex? What are you doing in there? I need you out front!" His mother. Hell.

Alex exhales and rubs a hand through his hair. "Be right there." He picks up the Indigo T-shirt that has fallen on the floor in the excitement. He leans over and whispers in my ear, "Please put this on before I get into trouble."

My skin tingles. "Thank you," I whisper back, trying to suppress a smile. "I would hate for you to get into trouble." I pull the shirt over my head. "There." I find my own soup-stained shirt on the floor where I'd dropped it.

Alex stares at me and frowns. "You'll still be cold. Here,

take this." He grabs his olive-green army surplus jacket, which is draped around the back of a chair.

I'm silent as he helps me into his jacket, suddenly a little dizzy as I'm wrapped in his scent. I can't help but sniff one of the cuffs. Gain and fresh-baked bread.

Alex gives me a look. "Can we talk later? I have to get back to work before I get fired, but I . . . we . . . I want to talk."

I nod. Would his moms really fire him?

"Great. I get off at ten. If that's not too late."

I finally find my voice. "I'll be up."

"Good. Great." He opens the door and looks out for his moms. No one is in sight, so I hurry back out to the front, where I grab my book bag and purse. Only Hank is still sitting in our booth. Trista must be in the bathroom with Natalie.

"Need a ride home?" Hank asks me. He's staring at his phone, but it's sweet of him to offer.

Please don't say anything about Alex's jacket. "No, I'd like to walk. But thanks. Tell Tris and Natalie I'll talk to them tomorrow?"

"Will do."

"Thanks." I leave as fast as I can, not bothering to look around for Alex. I don't want to see him right now. I definitely don't want to see either of his moms right now. All I want right now is to get out of here and get some fresh air. I need to think.

CHAPTER 19

I walk slowly, taking a quieter street off Milledge, with less traffic. I don't want to have to pay too much attention to where I'm going. I want to remember every second of Alex's kiss. My kiss. I did kiss him first, after all, and oh my God, what does he think of me now? He seemed to enjoy it, but what if he was just being nice?

That is probably what he wants to talk about. I'm certain he didn't appreciate being mauled by the girl with epilepsy and wants to make sure it never happens again. Maybe I'm a horrible kisser, and it will give him nightmares. I don't want to be the cause of any nightmares. Or of scarring someone for life.

But I am a terrible person. He was my twin sister's boyfriend. He's not ready for dating again. I took advantage of him and kissed him because I wanted to. I wanted him. And that is one of the most selfish things I've ever done.

Before I realize it, I'm already turning on to Azalea Cove, and before long, I see our driveway. Mom's car is gone. She must still be at the office. I dig my key from the bottom of my purse and unlock the door.

Sophie is waiting for me, but with less than her normal tail wagging and enthusiastic jumping around. "I love you too," I say, reaching down to scratch her ears. She follows me through the kitchen to the back door, where I let her out into the yard.

I grab a can of Diet Coke from the fridge and follow her outside. I can see that Mom has been digging in the flower beds today, probably trying to distract herself from everything going on with Craig. The wheelbarrow has been left out, along with a stack of huge bags of mulch and compost. Looks like she only got as far as weeding out the dead plants from last year. The sprayer that she uses to fumigate the yard for fleas every spring is lying on the ground. I pick it up and set it on the wheelbarrow.

She has never been content to keep just the front yard looking nice. The backyard has always looked like a magazine cover too. Sweeping beds full of annuals and flowering shrubs. A patch of white heavily scented flowers surrounding a gazebo in the back corner for a moon garden. Even the patio has perfectly arranged large pots of flowers and a few palm trees to sit under.

Sophie brings me an old favorite toy, her blue squeaky. I toss it across the yard for her to chase.

She brings it back, slowly this time, as I let her lie down at my feet to catch her breath. "Good girl," I say, letting her keep the squeaky for a while.

But she's not ready to go back inside when I get up.

She looks at me and lays her head back down on top of her paws.

"Sophie?"

Her only answer is a soft whimper.

My heart starts to pound as I slip into panic mode. She's almost as old as I am. And she's been moving much more slowly over the years, but I'm not ready to give her up just yet.

"Sophie!" I cry, dropping to my knees beside her.

She answers by coughing up a large amount of greenish foam. I get up and rush inside to call Mom. If Sophie has eaten something she shouldn't have, she'll need to go to the vet. When I was ten, she ate a bouquet of daisies, along with the packet of water purifier that came with it. She threw up green stuff just like this.

The phone is on the counter in the kitchen. I dial Mom's office and then her cell without waiting to leave a message at either.

I'm debating calling 911, when the doorbell rings.

I fling open the door, hoping to God it's Mom and she's forgotten her keys.

But it's Alex, leaning against the porch rail with a large paper bag from Indigo Dragon.

"Hey," he begins nervously. "I figured you might still be hungry, so I took off early and packed up some extra soup and a sandwich for you. . . ."

I grab his arm and pull him inside. "Did you bring your truck? We have to hurry." He follows me through the house as I grab an old soft towel from the hall closet.

"What's wrong?" he asks, immediately dumping the bag of food on the counter in the kitchen. "Are you okay?"

"No, it's Sophie! She's throwing up and my mom is not answering the phone and I can't drive." I open the back door and step onto the porch where Sophie is lying.

"Just slow down," Alex says, placing both hands on my shoulders. "Take a deep breath."

"I have to get her to the vet," I tell him, trying very hard not to cry. My voice gets wobbly, but I swallow hard. "They keep late hours. On Mondays and Wednesdays, they're open until eight."

"Which vet?" he asks, lifting Sophie gently in his arms.

"The one in the peach-colored cottage on Cypress. Just a short distance from here." I follow him out to his truck with her squeaky toy.

Alex's face looks grim as we fly through the suburbs, and each time I look down, Sophie is looking back at me with an incredibly sad gaze. My stomach twists into tiny knots. I can't lose her. Not today, not this month. Not ever.

The vet's office has a side door they keep open during late-night hours. I open the door while Alex carries my dog into the examination room.

Our vet is a smiling woman with short spiky white hair. But her smile falls when she sees what a pitiful dog I have. "Oh my goodness," she says. "What happened to you, Sophie?"

"I don't know. She was throwing up green stuff and not acting right. Not her normal self."

The vet examines Sophie swiftly. "I'm going to take a few labs, and give her some fluids. We'll get to the bottom of this."

"Thank you," I tell Dr. Rivers gratefully.

"Why don't you two have a seat out in the waiting room while I have a look at her?"

Alex pulls me away from Sophie. "Come on," he says. "You need to give the doctor room to work."

I follow him to the waiting room and sit down on a hard orange chair. An old episode of *The Big Bang Theory* plays on the TV. Alex reaches over and squeezes my hand. I squeeze back gratefully, and lay my head against his shoulder.

It seems like it was a lifetime ago that we were making out in his moms' café. It feels like it was all a dream. Like it wasn't really us.

"How old is your dog?" he asks.

"Almost twelve."

He nods. "She's just a puppy. She's going to be fine."

I take a deep breath. The tears that have been threatening to fall for the past hour finally pour out. My chest hurts because I am sobbing so hard.

Alex's arm slides around me, and I turn my face into his shoulder. His hand slides up and down my back as he tries to soothe me. "Hey, she's going to be fine. You are going to be fine."

I feel his lips close to my hair as he comforts me. I close my eyes, wanting nothing more than to remain in his arms like this for the rest of the night.

And then I pull away to stare at him. "I'm so sorry for dragging you into this. You didn't deserve to be turned into a pet transport."

He frowns as he looks at me. "You didn't drag me into anything. I'm here because you need me."

He's rendered me speechless. I do need him. I can't believe I'm admitting this. I don't like to need people. But it feels like letting out a long-held breath. Like falling and knowing someone is there to catch you.

"Andria?" The vet comes out into the waiting room, rubbing alcohol foam into her hands. "Sophie is going to be fine, but I want to keep her here overnight for some IV fluids."

"What's wrong with her?" I ask.

"It looks like she just got a little bit dehydrated. Maybe she got into something she shouldn't have. But she's going to be all right. Have you gotten in touch with your mother yet?"

I shake my head. "I sent her a text, though. She should be here soon."

Dr. Rivers nods. "We can take care of the paperwork tomorrow when you come to pick Sophie up. Want to come back and say good-night to her?"

Alex is holding my hand, and I squeeze his fingers, begging him silently to come with me. He understands. We both follow Dr. Rivers back into the kennel.

Sophie is whimpering in a crate along the bottom row. A Maltese in the cage above her growls softly. I drop down to the floor and stick my fingers up to Sophie's cage. She gives me a halfhearted lick.

"I'll see you in the morning," I say, trying not to cry in front of her. I don't know if it helps or not, but she looks so sad it is breaking my heart. "Just think of this as being a sleepover with the Maltese up there," I tell her. "When you come home tomorrow you can tell me all about the fun you two have had."

Alex squats down beside me. "They'll be up all night doing each other's hair and giggling about Justin Bieber."

I elbow him in the side. "Sophie is NOT a Belieber." I don't tell him that I named my dog after my favorite Diana Wynne Jones character. Even though I got Sophie as a puppy twelve years ago, long before Alex ever thought of naming a band Calcifer. Still, he doesn't need to know.

I sigh. "I'm not sure how I'm going to sleep without her. She stays next to my bed every night, watching out for seizures."

He puts a hand on my waist, and gives me a gentle squeeze. A friendly squeeze.

We hear the high heels before we hear Mom's voice. Just enough time for Alex to stand up and take a step away from me before she pushes the door open. "Andria? I'm so sorry, baby. I've been tied up at the office."

"It's fine. Alex brought us. Did Dr. Rivers tell you what's wrong?"

"Yes." She looks from me to Alex, and her face pales. "Alex? Hammond?"

He is looking at me, ignoring my mother. "Are you going to be okay?"

I nod. "Thank you." I want him to stay. I want him to realize we never talked about what we were supposed to talk about this evening. The kiss at the Indigo.

But I know he can feel the hostility coming off my mother in waves. She still sees him as the demonic influence of evil that killed Iris. "I'll see you tomorrow?" I ask.

He gives me the slightest of nods. "Take care." Then he gives Mom a little wave before walking out. I hope she can keep her mouth shut at least until he leaves. He doesn't need to hear the awful things I know she's going to say.

She doesn't wait. Her voice is shrill and tight. I'm certain he can hear her in the waiting room. "What the hell was he doing here with you?" Everyone in the vet's office can probably hear her.

I'm sure this isn't the right time to talk to her about Alex. "He's a friend."

Her eyes are brimming with pain. "How can you call that boy a friend? After what he did to Iris?"

I shake my head. "I think Iris was a bad influence on Alex."

But she is not in the mood to hear this right now. "I don't want that boy hanging around you."

"But he helped me get Sophie here. Where were you? I tried and tried to get hold of you. I was terrified that Sophie was dying and I didn't know where you were."

Mom's face crumples. "I'm so sorry, Andria. I came as soon as I saw your message."

Mom sighs and doesn't speak to me again until she's talked with the vet and we are back in her car, driving home again.

"Andria, I had things I had to do at work. I'm already losing clients since Craig was arrested. Do you know how much money a good divorce attorney costs?"

Of course I don't know, but I don't bother to point that out. She's ready to cut him out of our life, but I haven't thought about what she has to do legally to make that happen. I haven't stopped to consider the fact that we are now a one-income family. Of course Mom is worried about money.

I feel bad for adding to her stress. "I'm sorry. I didn't think about how much taking Sophie to the vet would cost."

"Oh, honey, do not worry about that. I'm sorry that I married an evil bastard who preys on young girls," she says bitterly. "What kind of person does that make me?"

But Craig had charmed everyone. He'd seemed to be the perfect husband, soccer coach, businessman, community leader.

Not a good stepfather.

Mom has not gone to visit Craig in jail, and I heard her refuse a collect call from him last night. One of her friends is a lawyer, but Ms. Helen specializes in real estate litigation, so she could only recommend a few names. And even though Mom has known Ms. Helen for years, I don't think they're close enough for Mom to tell her all the details of our family melodrama.

Mom picks up chicken salads for us at the local deli on our way home. She makes sure I take my meds and then disappears into her bedroom with a glass of wine.

I finish my homework and get ready for bed, but my room feels empty without Sophie. I turn out the light and lie down on my side, wishing I could hear her noisy snoring at the foot of my bed.

The cell phone on my nightstand lights up. It's a text from Alex. *Are you okay?*

My heart grows warm and tingly. Now I am. I text back *Yes* and curl myself around my phone, cradling it in my hand.

It glows again.

Our share of night to bear . . .

I can't help but smile at my screen. The depressing poetry of Miss Emily Dickinson. I've finally converted him.

Here a star, and there a star/ Some lose their way, I text back.

I've missed our poetry. It seems like we can say so much more to each other when we use other people's words.

Afterwards—day! (See you in the morning.)

I think my face is probably glowing brighter than my phone screen. I text back a smiley face, something I haven't used in a text in months.

I get a smiley face back. My dark bedroom doesn't seem quite so empty anymore.

CHAPTER 20

Four Days

The clock says 3:52 when I wake up. I know I was dreaming about Iris, but I can't remember what it was about. I'm tired of the dreams of her trying to tell me something when I can't hear her, or understand her, or see her. It's so frustrating. And maybe that's what the dreams mean. I'm frustrated that I didn't see or hear anything going on in her life until it was too late. I can't hear her in my dreams because I never heard her crying out for help in real life.

Worst sister ever.

I drag myself out of bed, automatically trying to avoid stepping on a sleeping dog that isn't there. My heart hurts. I won't be able to call and check on Sophie for another four hours.

I want to make coffee, but I don't want to argue with Mom again. So I settle for a can of Diet Coke. I know she's not sleeping very well either lately. Both with the absence of a body in the bed beside her, as well as the absence of the CPAP noise. Tonight I've learned all about trying to sleep with silence.

And sure enough. Moments after I pop my can open, she is shuffling into the kitchen.

She yawns as she ties her robe shut. "Andria? What are you doing?"

"Can't sleep. I thought I'd go outside with the telescope."

She grabs a can of Diet Coke from the fridge and leans back against the counter. Her eyes look puffy. Either she drank more than the one glass of wine last night or she cried herself to sleep. I'm not sure which makes me unhappier.

She stares at me, and I know she is wondering, worrying.

I roll my eyes. "No, Craig never touched me."

She looks relieved. "Baby, if he did, you can tell me."

But would she really want to know? I think she would be equally relieved if I had been abused and just denied it.

"And no, Iris never said anything to me," I add, before she opens her mouth to ask. "Or I would have just killed him and hidden the body."

She sighs. "That's not funny."

"We should tell the police about the diary," I say.

"No. It won't bring her back, and the cops should already have enough evidence to keep that bastard in jail."

"But it might be good for Kimber to know she wasn't alone," I say.

Mom sets her can of Diet Coke down on the counter, hard. "No. I don't want to turn our lives inside out for everyone to see. You don't need to put up with that at school, and I don't need it at work either."

Right. "Because it's bad enough that the house on Azalea Cove with the Garden of the Year was the residence of a pedophile. We don't want anyone to know what he was doing here behind closed doors."

She glares at me, and I feel like a bitch. I know she's trying to protect us, but I believe she should do the right thing.

And I can't fathom how she's dealing with all of this.

"Anything pretty to look at tonight?" she asks me. This is how she deals. Changing the subject. She is trying to be Best Friend Mom now.

I shrug. "Just haven't looked in a while. The moon already set hours ago, so the sky should be dark."

She looks me over from head to toe. "Just make sure you dress warmly. I'm going to try and get some more sleep."

I'm wearing a long-sleeved black T-shirt and fuzzy Hello Kitty pajama pants. I think I'll be fine. "I'll get my slippers."

She shakes her head and takes her canned drink back to her bedroom. I leave mine beside the sink. I grab a bottle of water from the fridge instead.

After I get my slippers and throw on a hoodie just in case, I take the telescope into the front yard, down to the end of the driveway.

I tell myself it's to see the Pleiades better, even though they've already sunk too far into the west behind the trees. I tell myself I'm not hoping someone will come jogging down my dead-end street at four o'clock in the morning. I tell myself I put on strawberry lip gloss because it's very chilly outside and I don't want my lips to get chapped.

My cell phone is in my hoodie pocket, back on silent. I fight the urge to text Alex. If he's sleeping, then I don't want to wake him.

But while I'm turning my telescope toward the northeast, and finding the three stars of Orion's Belt, I hear footsteps and heavy, rhythmic breathing. Instead of being afraid, I feel relief. And excitement.

Of course it's him.

The street lights are sparse on Azalea Cove, so when he passes under the one three houses down, I can just make out his bare arms and legs. He's wearing a sleeveless black T-shirt and running shorts. Not his typical Alexwear.

But I recognize him by the short close-cropped hair. As he gets closer, I see he's wearing earbuds, but he looks up at me.

I step away from my telescope to protect it and stuff my hands in my front pockets. He slows down as he approaches, coming to a stop inches from me. I can smell his body heat, hear his heavy breathing as he bends over, hands on his knees, as he catches his breath. His hair and forehead are damp from sweat. His arms are slick.

"Aren't you cold out here?" I ask, shivering in sympathy even though I'm comfortable in my hoodie.

He shakes his head.

"Are you sure? I can go inside and get your jacket from my bedroom."

He reaches out as if to grab my arm, to touch me, but then doesn't. "Stay. I'm fine."

"Want some water?" I pick up the bottle I'd set down on the ground next to my telescope.

"Oh God, that would be wonderful." He takes it from me, and I watch his throat in the dim light as he swallows. He wipes his forehead with his bare arm. But already the chilly air is drying the sweat from his skin.

Alex is here, in front of me. And I'm looking at him not like a villain but as some sort of hero. He's larger-than-life Alex again. I feel very small again. But not shy. I stare at him as he finishes the bottle.

"Couldn't sleep either?" I ask.

He grins and sets the empty bottle down on the ground. "No. You?"

I shake my head.

"I'm sorry you had to sleep alone last night," he says.

It takes me a minute to realize he's talking about Sophie. "Your texts helped. Hopefully she'll get to come home today. Thank you again for everything you did last night."

He looks away. His forehead wrinkles, and it looks like I've said the wrong thing.

"Want to see something beautiful?" I wave my hand belatedly toward the telescope. I don't want him to think I'm talking about myself.

He takes a step closer to me and is looking down at me. He's smiling again, and that makes me happy. "Show me what you've got."

I take a peek to make sure Alnitak is still lined up. The Horsehead Nebula rises up from a glittery rainbow-colored cloud. I move to let Alex see.

He bends his head down to look. I forgot to adjust for his height. "Sorry, I can raise it up some," I say.

He doesn't bother to move. "Don't worry about it." He's silent for a moment, and I know he is seeing his first nebula. "Holy shit," he whispers.

I smile up into the darkness. These are my stars. And I am sharing them with you, Alex Hammond.

He reaches out without looking away from the telescope. His fingers lace into mine, and I hold on for dear life. "Beautiful," he whispers.

Baby stars being born fifteen hundred light-years away. I wish I could show Alex what the nebula looks like from a Hubble photograph. With my lens you can just make out the horsehead shape, but the pictures I've seen online are breathtaking.

"I guess it's worth a few sleepless nights when you get to see something like this?" he asks, finally turning away from the telescope.

I shrug. "I used to think so."

His eyes grow sad again. "I understand. I don't look forward to running in the middle of the night when I can't sleep, but I figured I'd put my insomnia to good use."

"No more nightmares?" I ask. "Just can't sleep?"

He still has my hand in his, and he leads me up the driveway to a bench under the oak tree. Here we're hidden from the neighbor's porch, as well as from my mother's bedroom window.

"No nightmares," he whispers, his mouth very close to my ear. "I just couldn't get you out of my head."

Before I can say anything, Alex turns my face to his and kisses me. The world starts to spin.

He's not larger than life anymore. He's my poet, my patron saint, a Greek demigod. But he's also just Alex, and he's kissing me like his life depends on it.

Like my life depends on it.

He shivers, and I think he's getting cold. My fingertips run up his arms and across his shoulders. "Are you sure you don't want your jacket?" I murmur. Not that I want to go anywhere right this moment.

He pulls me against him, and I don't resist. His lips brush the side of my neck, and I feel like purring. The sound I do make causes him to laugh as he nips my earlobe. His hands slide down to my hips and stay there, not sneaking down into my pants or up under my top. But he groans when I throw my legs around his hips and twist so I'm basically sitting in his lap, straddling him.

I'm not thinking about what I'm doing to him. I'm only trying to get closer. To close the distance between our bodies.

"God, woman," he whispers, his forehead resting on mine. "When did you become such a wicked little minx?"

This makes me giggle, in a very un-wicked way. "I can't get you out of my head, either."

With a sigh, he pulls back a little so I can see his eyes. "I shouldn't be here. I wish I could stay away from you."

I put a hand on his chest. Over his thumping heart. "But I'm glad you're here. I don't want you to stay away."

He's silent, but I can hear and feel his deep breathing. His hands are still on my hips, and I think as long as he holds on to me, we're okay.

"God, I'm such a bastard," he finally says.

"What are you talking about?" He's still touching me, but I'm losing him. The fire in his eyes has dimmed.

"I don't deserve you. Not after everything I've done. All the mistakes I've made."

I put my hand across his mouth. "Stop talking like that."

He stares at me with pain in his eyes. His hand moves to take my hand, and he kisses my fingers before moving them away from his mouth.

"Why couldn't we have gotten together two years ago? Our lives would have turned out so differently."

Before he started dating Iris. I pull my hand out of his.

He sighs. "We can't be together, Andria. It's not fair to you. Or to me."

Oh God. A cold black hole opens up in my stomach. It sucks the last traces of warmth and fuzzy happiness from my body. This has been too good to be true. I was dreaming to think he could care about me.

"You still love her," I manage to whisper. I don't want him to know how close I am to crying. Even dead, my sister still has everything I've ever wanted. I am so close to hating Iris right now.

"What? God, no." Alex frowns as he realizes what is going through my head. He grabs my hips again and picks me up off him, setting me down gently on the bench. "Listen to me. You deserve someone much better than me. Someone less fucked-up. Someone who never caused the pain I've caused you."

He leans over me and presses his lips against my forehead. But the warmth and fuzziness doesn't come back. This kiss feels final. A good-bye.

"No matter what you think right this moment, Andria,

you'll never be able to forgive me for Iris's death. It will always be between us."

He takes off jogging again, without another glance back. I stare at him until he disappears into the shadows under the oak trees at the end of the street. Pride keeps me from running after him. And my shock and grief begin to turn into anger.

I grab the empty water bottle off the driveway and crumple it, but resist the urge to throw it across the yard. How dare he be so self-sacrificing? It's not up to him whether I can forgive him or not. And maybe I already have, I realize furiously, and I haven't had the chance to tell him.

I stomp over to my telescope to start packing things up. What if he is right? Will I always harbor resentment for the things he used to do? Will I always worry that he'll relapse? Will I be able to trust him? He's changed so much since he came back from rehab, but what if he hasn't changed enough? Was he telling the truth when he said he wasn't still in love with Iris?

Any tears that threatened to fall earlier are long gone. I should be weeping for this beautiful boy who keeps pushing me away, but instead I'm pissed. He has no right to decide what I deserve or what I don't deserve. What I should want or not want.

I take one last look up into the sky before carrying my stuff inside. The three stars of Orion's Belt twinkle on, oblivious to what's going on down here below. And I know fifteen hundred light-years away, stars are still being born and stars are still dying. The universe doesn't give a damn about what I want. But dear God, Alex, all I want is you.

CHAPTER 21

Three Days

WR 136 is a dying star. It's 4.5 million years old and is at the center of the Crescent Nebula. This nebula was created by the stellar wind of the star exploding into a red supergiant hundreds of thousands of years ago. It is believed that WR 136 will end its final days as a supernova, sometime in the next million years.

I'm reading about the Crescent Nebula in a new astrophotography magazine that Verla ordered for me. A photo of this star explosion won an observatory photo-of-the-year contest in England. It looks like a giant heart. A heart that is twenty five light-years across.

"That is absolutely gorgeous," Verla says, leaning over my shoulder. "Have you ever submitted photos for contests like this?"

I laugh. "My telescope would never be able to see something like that. I'd have to use one of the big ones, like at a university."

She looks at me over her glasses. "Are you going to UGA?"

I shrug. "They do have a pretty good observatory. I'd love to go to Cornell or maybe somewhere out in California, but my mother's afraid of me going too far away." And now with Craig gone, I don't want to go too far away from her either.

Verla smiles. "You are very smart, Andria. You hit some bumps this year, but you've managed to pull yourself out of the hole you dug. You could get into any college you wanted."

But I didn't dig that hole all by myself. And what I always thought I wanted might not be what I want now. And what if the things I'd always wanted are all wrong for me?

I stare at the giant exploding heart in its flurry of glorious colors. Turquoise and pink. I love the fact that something so beautiful was caused by something so violent as a suicidal star.

I'm hiding in the library before school. I dread seeing Trista and Natalie this morning in chemistry. And I dread seeing Alex. I don't want my friends knowing Alex and I are doing . . . whatever it is we're doing. Or were doing. That we were doing something and now we aren't doing anything.

I don't even want to think about it anymore.

I slink into class at the last minute, but I'm still ambushed. Natalie grabs my med alert bracelet the moment I sit down in my seat in first block. She's so excited she almost snaps the bracelet off my wrist.

"Ouch," I say, rubbing my skin.

"Sorry! Last week of license-less-ness!"

"That is not even a word. But hopefully," I say. I've grown superstitious over the past few months. I don't want anything to screw this up. I might have gone a little overboard with the caffeine, but I've been diligent about taking my pills. I've even studied the driving handbook a few extra times. I'm so close now, I don't know what I'll do if something happens and I can't get my license.

I'll have Sophie back at home with me this evening. Mom told me this morning she'd pick her up from the vet's before she went in to work.

She's still planning to go to the office in the afternoon, when no one else is there, but soon she's going to have to start dealing with other people. She's going to have to deal with Craig's contractors. And show houses to people. Eventually Craig's trial will go to trial and he'll be sentenced and people will forget about him. And she'll forget that she ever had to sleep with the sound of his CPAP machine droning in her ears. And I think she'll be okay. Eventually.

Natalie and Trista are sticking close to me, but I notice none of the other soccer girls talk to me, or even look at me if they can help it. I'm not upset about it. But I wonder how soon the trial will begin. If Kimber will have to testify.

I know Mom's been on the phone with Craig's attorney, because she refused to let Craig return to our house when he was released on bail. Not even to get any of his things. She stuffed all of his clothes in garbage bags and dumped them off at his office. All photographs of him and her have been taken down. All of his soccer things have been put into totes and placed in the garage. I'm sure he'll want that stuff one day.

Mom sold his motorcycle to pay for her divorce attorney. She thinks the divorce will be finalized before his case goes to trial. She says that could take over a year. By then, will Kimber still remember what happened to her? Will her story change? Will anyone besides Kimber and her family care?

Mom did not want to turn over Iris's diary to the police. She does not want our family being dragged into this any more if possible. She doesn't want to have to talk to anyone else about Iris's death. It would be like losing my sister all over again. And Mom does not like airing family dirty laundry. Craig has been cut off from our family. Clean, like a surgeon's slice. To bring Iris's confessions out into the open would show the world just how fucked-up our family really was. Mom can't have that. Better to let people believe that Craig only had sex with someone else's teenage daughter and let him go to jail for that.

But it makes me sick to my stomach to hear several girls at school defend the asshole, while they think Kimber is making the story up. Why would she?

There's something scribbled in pencil across the top of my desk in algebra. My heart thumps out of control so suddenly it's embarrassing. Stupid flopping thing. I know realistically no one else can hear it, but I feel self-conscious anyway.

> *Places among the stars,*
> *Soft gardens near the sun,*
> *Keep your distant beauty;*
> *Shed no beams upon my weak heart.*
> *Since she is here*
> *In a place of blackness,*
> *Not your golden days*
> *Nor your silver nights*
> *Can call me to you.*
> *Since she is here*
> *In a place of blackness,*
> *Here I stay and wait*

I copy the lines along the side of the homework Mrs. Davis has just handed back. My handwriting stretches across the 76 written on the top of the page in red ink. Does he really think we're both standing in darkness? Or is he still thinking about Iris?

Sadness creeps into my chest cavity. No, that's not right. It's always there, lurking. But at the moment I'm unable to hold it back. It breaches the dam, flooding everything and destroying everything in its path.

Dammit. I squeeze my eyes shut, determined not to let anyone else see this storm surge.

As soon as class is over, I take the paper to the library to borrow a computer and look up the lines.

The library is full of project boards, entries into Athens High School's First Annual Poetry Fair. Verla is giggling as she wanders out from the forest of cardboard. "Isn't this great? I'm so excited we got so many participants! Where is yours?"

"I'm kinda poetried out right now," I say. "I'll do one next year."

Verla shakes her head. "One can never overdose on poetry."

She doesn't notice me flinch at the word "overdose."

"Hey, could a project give me extra credit in algebra?" I ask.

"Ha. Do you know the begging and pleading involved in getting the English department to okay extra credit? Why aren't you doing well in algebra? Do you need a tutor?"

I shake my head as I find my way to a free computer. I pass by large boards with images of Shakespeare and Maya Angelou and Robert Frost. "I'll be fine. Just need to put more effort into my homework." I Google the lines that Alex left me. They're by Stephen Crane. "Places Among the Stars."

I remember Alex cataloging Crane's book last week. I pull my phone out of my bag and send him a message.

Just what are you waiting for in the darkness?

Verla bursts out laughing somewhere among the poetry fair projects.

"Are you okay?" I ask, gathering my stuff back up.

"Come here!" she says. "I love this one. Too bad I have to disqualify it."

"What?" I follow the sound of her voice and find her in front of a black tri-board, covered with words in metallic silver Sharpie. I cock my head sideways to read all the lines. "It's a U2 song."

Verla shrugs. "I mean, I get that this student wants us to think of Bono as a modern poet. But the rules specifically said no song lyrics. I love the handwriting. And I love that song," she says with a sigh.

I'm still staring at the board when the library doors open. I glance down at my phone, but there's been no reply from Alex.

"Excuse me? Hello?" A man is making his way through the displays, and I see boards wobble in his wake.

Verla waves her hands in the air. "This way," she calls out.

When he reaches us, I see he's younger than I first thought. A college student, maybe. His black hair is shoulder length, and I notice Verla checking him out. That makes me smile.

"Hi, I was told I could find Andria Webb here?"

Verla takes a protective step in front of me. Is he a cop? Someone from the media? Mom warned me that reporters might try to talk to me, but so far I've been ignored.

"My name is Collin Coleman. I'm Alex Hammond's AA sponsor, and I was wondering if I could talk with Andria about Alex."

All of a sudden I know where I've seen him before. He was coming out of the church with Alex that day I saw him. "That's me," I say.

Collin fidgets with something in his hand, then moves his hands to his pockets. "He's been skipping meetings lately and I'm worried about him. You know, relationships are usually frowned upon during the first twelve months of sobriety, because it puts an added stress on the recovering addict."

I shake my head. "We don't have a relationship. You have nothing to worry about there."

Collin crosses his arms. It's like he just doesn't know what to do with his hands. "I know the two of you have grown close. He's told me about your sister, Iris. My condolences."

I cross my arms too. So does Verla. "Does Alex know you're here?" she asks.

"I asked him if he wanted to invite you to an AA meeting, Andria. I think it might help you understand his struggle better. It might help you understand your sister better as well."

He holds out a business card. "Here's a list of the times of our open meetings. Maybe Alex will come back if you offer to come with him."

I take the card. It lists the address of the Lutheran church on Broad. "I don't know how much of an influence I can be."

Collin smiles, but it's halfhearted. "Much greater than you think." He really seems troubled. I don't see him as the type of wise old sponsor bestowing calm nuggets of wisdom to anyone. "Hope to see both you and Alex soon," he says as he turns to go.

Collin leaves, and Verla looks at me, her arms still crossed. "Want to talk?"

I roll my eyes. "Thank you, but no. There's nothing to talk about. Unless you have any more books that need cataloging?"

She doesn't move. "Are you going to go with Alex to a meeting? They have another group specifically for family members of addicts."

"I don't have any addicts in my family." I scowl. Not anymore.

Verla sighs and throws her arm around me. "I know, hon. But you still have to deal with the feelings your sister caused. She's gone, but those feelings are still there."

"I've already dealt with them."

DREAMING OF ANTIGONE   147

"Did your mom ever let you talk to a counselor?"

I want to laugh. "Of course not." That would have been the same as admitting emotional weakness or instability. Mom believes we as a family mourned for an appropriate amount of time and then we all moved on.

"And that guy was right. They really do frown upon new relationships when an addict's recovery is still fragile. But I think you and Alex might help each other heal."

I stare at my librarian. "You're such a romantic."

She shrugs. "And I'm no therapist, so take my advice with a grain of salt. Or a whole salt shaker."

"Will do." My phone vibrates in my pocket, and I pull it out, expecting a text from Mom. It's from Alex instead. *I'm waiting for you to wake up and find someone better. You're the type of girl who deserves someone who makes you happy.*

I don't think that it's up to you to decide what or who makes me happy, I text back. I want to ask where he is, but I don't want to sound like a stalker. *I miss you,* I type, and my finger pauses over the "Send" button. It's only been two days since that morning we talked in my yard, but I go ahead and send the text, holding my breath.

There's no reply.

Dammit. I shouldn't have told him that. He already thinks I'm emotionally needy.

I stare at the phone for another minute.

Still no reply.

Dammit.

Verla turns out the lights, blanketing the library in late-afternoon darkness. "Are you coming?" she asks from the door. "I need to lock up."

"Be right there." I put my phone in my hoodie pocket and grab my backpack. The weight of the phone hits me over and over as I follow Verla out into the school parking lot.

"Need a ride?" she asks, her key ring spinning around her finger.

"Nope, my mom is parked over there," I say, pointing to the silver Lexus.

"Are you going to ask her about going to the AA meeting?"

I shrug. That is not a conversation that would go well. "We'll see."

"See you tomorrow then," she says, turning away.

I watch her walk away, unhappy knowing that I'm disappointing her. She wants me to heal, and do the fuzzy, warm healing stuff with a counselor so I can be better and help fix Alex.

Mom's frowning over her phone when I get into the car. "What's wrong?" I ask.

"Nothing. Craig has been calling, wanting the rest of his things. I'm just not in the mood to deal with him right now."

"How is Sophie doing?"

"She's fine and she'll be happy to see you. She curled up at the foot of your bed as soon as I got her home."

My phone vibrates against my belly and I jump a little. I take it out to read three little words that mean everything to me: *Miss you too.* It takes everything I possess not to make Mom turn the car around and search the school for Alex. He misses me. I have to be content with that for the moment.

Sophie jumps up, wagging her tail like a puppy as soon as I open my bedroom door. I drop to the floor and give her a hug, thankful that she's okay. "It's you and me, girl," I whisper into her fur. Ugh, she smells like the clinic. Like medicine and urine. Like hospitals and death. Before I start on any homework, she needs a bath.

I find her lavender-scented dog shampoo out in the garage and bring it up to my bathroom. Mom has kittens when I bathe Sophie in my tub, but it's too cold outside for a bath. I hope I can bathe her and clean the tub before Mom notices. I won't be able to sleep tonight if I can't get the smell of sickness off her.

Alex said he misses me. I keep telling myself I'm content with that, but it's not contentment that warms the space inside my rib cage with fluffy bunny feelings. I think it's something more than that. And I think I want something more than contentment from him as well.

CHAPTER 22

I wash and dry Sophie off, then have to take a shower myself to get the veterinarian smell off me. When we are both feeling pretty and daisy fresh, I attach her leash to her collar and take her outside for a walk. The vet told me to keep up her exercise, even if we can't do the five- or seven-mile walks we used to do. Sophie's tail wags hopefully as I get her ready for an outing.

I tell Mom where we're going and reassure her that I have my phone on me. "Be back before dark," she says, kissing me on the forehead.

Now I smell like her perfume. I feel like I need another shower.

"I was thinking we could go to the movies tomorrow night and have dinner at your favorite Japanese place?"

Now is the right time to bring up the AA meeting, which is also tomorrow night. But I chicken out. And Mom needs me just as much as Alex does. "Sounds like fun."

She beams, and I feel like I've made the right decision. "Great!"

Sophie is tugging on her leash, so I let her outside and she pulls me toward the sidewalk. She loves our walks. She's a well-behaved husky who likes receiving attention from our neighbors. But it's getting close to dinnertime, so her favorites aren't outdoors to wave to her or offer her treats.

We start off briskly toward the main road, and Sophie is all no-nonsense. She doesn't stop to sniff mailboxes or pee anywhere. And then we get to the end of our dead-end street, and she starts pulling north. I'd planned to go south, toward Hydrangea Lane, but she has other ideas.

Pine Street is north of us. Where the Hammonds live. Sophie knows my heart better than I do. Or she has an evil, twisted mind and enjoys seeing me suffer. I'd like to think otherwise.

We turn down Pine Street. It's not like I expect to see him in his front yard. It's not like I plan to ring his doorbell and run away giggling like a twelve year old. I don't plan to do anything. We're taking a walk. Me and my dog. Enjoying the fresh air.

Alex lives five houses down from the end. The one directly behind our house. It's a beautiful two story that was built in 1905 and is on the historical register. I've always loved the broad porch that wraps around the front and side. The garage is a separate building that was added on recently.

There's music coming from the garage. Sophie's ears prick up, and she glances toward the sound of guitars. Calcifer is practicing again.

I hear Thing One's angry voice singing a song I recognize from the radio, though I don't know the band's name. Hank loves the angsty grunge rock groups of the nineties. Alex and Caleb have always been more eclectic in their tastes. I've heard them play Beatles songs, and I've heard them thrash out to Lady Gaga.

The garage doors are open, and I pray Sophie walks fast

enough that we pass by the Hammonds' without being noticed. The street is lined with old oak trees with low-hanging
branches, and it would be difficult for someone in the garage to
see a person walking down the shady street.

But Sophie barks when she hears Hank's feral guitar solo.
And suddenly the music stops.

Oh dear lord. I give her leash a little tug and say, "Come
on. You were the one who wanted to walk on this street."

Alex comes down his driveway, twirling his drumstick in
his hand. "She looks great! Did she come home today?"

I nod as he bends down to scratch her under her chin. Sophie
rolls over and presents her belly to him. "The band sounds great."

He looks up at me, and for the first time in months, I see a
real Alex Hammond smile. His eyes have a sparkly look that
wasn't there before. "Want to come listen? Will Sophie mind?"

His smile dazzles me, and I can't think or speak coherently
for a moment. "I don't think she likes Hank's guitar. And I
promised Mom we wouldn't be gone long."

I want to ask him about his AA mentor, and I want to ask
when he plans to go to another meeting. But he looks so
happy playing with Sophie. And Sophie is eating up the attention. I can't bring myself to talk about serious things and spoil
the moment.

"Pluto!" Hank shouts from inside the garage. "Quit flirting! You can hook up on your own time, man!"

Alex sighs and straightens back up. His blue eyes aren't
quite so sparkly anymore. "Bye, ladies. I guess I'll see you tomorrow."

"It looks like you're having fun. That's a good thing." I
want him to know that I want him to be happy. That it's okay
after all the shit we've both been through, that it's okay to be
happy. "See you tomorrow."

DREAMING OF ANTIGONE   153

Just as he turns back toward the garage, an orange El Camino pulls up along the street, its engine rumbling ominously.

The sparkle has completely disappeared from Alex's eyes as he glares at the vehicle. "You should probably go ahead with your walk, Andria."

Mike gets out of the car. Iris and Alex's drug dealer. Sophie feels the sudden tension surrounding her and growls softly. Alex reaches back down to reassure her, but she slinks closer to me.

My chest feels hollow inside, all the fuzzy, warm feelings completely drained out. I glance back up at Alex. His body is rigidly tense now, and the pain is back in his eyes. Mike is the one that can fix that pain for him.

"What the hell are you doing here?" Alex asks him.

"Been forever since I've seen you, Pluto. Missed you, friend."

"Sorry, but I haven't missed you. You need to leave. Now."

"Don't be so inhospitable. Your boys up there called me." He nods toward the garage. "Unless you need something too." Mike looks Alex up and down. "You look like you definitely need something. You are about to come apart, friend."

Alex does look like he's about to explode. The drug dealer knows how to read people. I'm almost in awe of him.

Almost.

"Let's go, Soph," I say quietly, and she quickly obeys. She is back in Seizure Guard Dog mode, ready to protect me.

"Hello, Beautiful," Mike says, looking me up and down. "You look like you could use a little something too. The world is too full of sadness. You don't need to suffer, though."

Sophie doesn't growl, but she knows I'm tense. The fur is standing up on her back. She keeps her eye on Mike.

"Leave her alone," Alex says. "Andria, go home."

I really don't like the way he's ordering me around. I was leaving anyway. But the rebellious, stubborn toddler inside me balks.

"Pluto!" Hank shouts again. "Quit pissing around! You and Mike need to come inside!"

Alex shakes his head. "You're leaving," he tells Mike. "Now, before I call the cops."

Mike grins and holds his hands up. "No need to get hostile, friend. Just tell Hank to come out to the car and check out my cookies." His smile is almost perfectly innocent. "Made a new batch, especially for him. But I'm sure he'll share with you if you're interested."

"Not going to happen," Alex says. He pulls his cell phone out of his back pocket.

"Okay!" Mike says, taking a step backward. "Jesus. Just tell Hank I'll see him at Nona in an hour. I'll be waiting there with his cookies."

That was my favorite restaurant. Was. Now I won't be able to enjoy it, knowing Mike uses it to sell his . . . cookies.

My stomach twists into knots as I remember it was Iris's favorite restaurant too. I guess it wasn't because she loved the eggplant parmesan as much as I do. Dammit, why do my sister and her drugs have to ruin everything?

"Calling 9 . . . 1 . . . 1 . . ." Alex says, pressing numbers on his screen.

"Leaving right now," Mike says, opening his car door. He gets in and starts his engine. "See you around, Beautiful," he says to me with a grin.

Alex holds his phone up to his ear until Mike drives off. But he never does call. As soon as the El Camino is around the corner, Alex slides his phone back in his jeans.

I turn Sophie around and tell her, "Come on, let's go home."

"Wait," Alex says. "I should probably walk you back, in case Mike tries anything." He sighs and runs his hands across the top of his head.

I wait, watching him. Sophie is being exceedingly impatient.

He takes a step back and looks toward the garage. "Or maybe Caleb should walk with you." He's torn between wanting to protect me and wanting to protect himself. He thinks he should stay away from me. Like I'm just as dangerous to him as the drug dealer.

"I'll be fine." I jerk the leash. "Come on, Soph."

And he doesn't say anything. No protests, no running after me. I walk away and don't look back. Maybe I am just as dangerous to him as Mike. Because I could make him happy, a real danger to his brooding and self-blame.

Sophie senses my urgency and trots briskly back to Azalea Cove. There's no sign of Mike. He's on his way to the restaurant and has money to make.

Mom is pulling a lentil casserole out of the oven when we get home. "Just in time," she says. "How is Sophie doing?"

"Much better. She enjoyed our walk." I'm glad Mom decided to cook tonight. It's been a while since she made us a home-cooked meal. I was worried she'd want to go out again. Possibly for Italian.

I hang Sophie's leash up and head to the bathroom to wash my hands for dinner. My phone vibrates. I pull it out of my pocket and set it on my dresser, the screen facing down. If it's Alex, I don't want to know. If it's not Alex, I don't want to know that either.

Mom is sitting at the table, twisting a wine glass by its stem. She has been drinking an awful lot of wine lately. Not that I catch her all the time, but I've seen far too many empty bottles in the recycling bin since Craig was arrested.

"How was your day?" she asks me.

"Fine. How was yours?" She's already fixed my plate: a

sweet potato and yellow lentil casserole with warm flat bread on the side. It smells spicy.

"Good. Tell me if you like this meal. It's an Ethiopian recipe I found online."

"It's yummy," I say, trying a bite.

Mom stares at the curtains. She's not touching her food.

"Don't you like it?" I ask, between shoveling spoonfuls into my mouth.

She sighs. "I've been thinking how much sadness there is in this house. Maybe we should move."

My spoon falls from my hand with a heavy clang. "Why? There's sadness everywhere, Mom. Sad things happen to us."

She smiles. "It does seem like we're cursed, doesn't it? First your dad, then Iris. And now the problems with Craig. Not to mention your seizures."

"My seizures aren't a curse. They're just something I live with. Like my black hair."

Mom's smile never breaks, but it grows brittle. "But you shouldn't have to live with them, dear. You deserve to be happy."

I want to growl but settle for pushing my plate away. She can't just wish away my seizures. She's always seen them as something that reflects on her personal failure as a mother. That obviously I won't ever be happy because I have epilepsy.

"And I deserve to be happy," Mom continues, draining her wine glass. "I think a new start in a new place would make me happy. My grandmother always used to say you should follow your bliss."

Mom's grandmother was from Greece, and she also used to say, "I will drink your blood!" when she thought someone had wronged her. She was a little crazy. Whether my mom and I deserve happiness or not, I don't think running away is going to help us find it.

Besides, moving would be like abandoning Iris's memory. This is where we grew up. There won't be any memories of her at a new house.

Maybe that's what Mom wants, though. She doesn't want to be haunted by images of Iris's abuse at Craig's hands. But leaving the house behind would just feel like pretending it didn't happen. And we have plenty of good memories that should cancel out the bad ones.

I wonder if you can exorcise a house of bad memories. But keep the good ones. We hardly ever use this dining room, usually eating in the kitchen or on the go. But we celebrate birthdays and entertain guests at this table. Mom always had two cakes for me and Iris: chocolate for Iris, carrot cake with cream cheese frosting for me.

This year I think I will want red velvet. But I still want to celebrate here. So I can still share my birthday with Iris. In our home.

Mom sighs. I don't know if it's because I don't want to move or because her wine glass is empty.

"I'm not talking about moving out of the school district. Just a new neighborhood. You'll still be able to graduate with your friends."

"It's not that," I say. "Iris lived here."

Mom looks at me, and for a split second I see pain in her eyes. And then the icy glare is back. She looks so much like Iris I would laugh if I didn't hurt so much for her. "But she doesn't live here now," she says softly. "And since she never will again, why should we bury ourselves in this house? We need to move on. We need to move."

I shake my head. I can't believe Mom is serious about this. "All the time and effort you've put into our house. Your garden is your pride and joy."

"I can always grow a new garden." She shrugs as she finally

gets up from the table. She takes her plate and mine and stacks them on top of one another, then picks up her empty glass. "I suppose I can wait until you leave for college in a few years. But I can't stay in this house much longer, Andria. The memories hurt too much."

CHAPTER 23

Two Days

I am superstitious this morning as I get dressed. Two days until my doctor's appointment, where she will sign the paper that allows me to take my driver's test. Two days left for something terrible to happen. I wear my lucky striped Wicked Witch of the West socks with my red Chuck Taylor's. I remember to take my medicine. I remember not to drink any coffee, even though I've been up all night worrying about Alex. The sleep I did get was ruined with nightmares about Iris.

I take the bus to school, leaving Mom asleep in her bed so I don't have to argue with her about moving again. I meet Natalie at the bus stop closest to Jittery Joe's. She offers me a sip from her cup. There is cinnamon-scented steam escaping out the top. Mmm. "No, thank you," I say, smiling wistfully.

"So, what time is your appointment?" she asks me as the bus pulls up.

"Nine. I'll probably check into algebra afterward."

"You'll get to sleep late," she says. "Lucky. You should talk your mom into just taking you straight to the DMV after the doctor gives you the paperwork. You could have your license before the weekend!"

She's jinxing me, I just know it. I hope she doesn't notice my shudder.

"And then we have to decide what we're doing this weekend. Don't worry about Trista. She knows you'd like to do something closer to home than Six Flags. So what about midnight miniature golf?"

I smile. Athens has an indoor glow-in-the-dark course, with late-night hours. "That sounds like fun."

"Yay!" Natalie grins, happy to see me excited about something for once. "Should we invite the boys?" She nods toward Alex's truck as it passes us by.

"No," I say, too quickly for it to sound polite.

Natalie's grin slips. "Oh, I thought . . . I was hoping . . ."

That we'd all be matched up with the band members, just like Pink Ladies and the T-Birds? I shrug. "No."

She doesn't say anything else for the rest of the ride to school. She stares out the window at the busy morning traffic, and her coffee grows cold.

And now I feel terrible.

As we descend the steps onto our campus, I finally relent. Natalie is a romantic. She's hoping Caleb will turn out not to be such a jerk after all, and that Alex and I can save each other from whatever demons she imagines we suffer from. And Trista and Hank will end up being the next Beyoncé and Jay Z.

"Okay," I tell her. "If you think the boys won't mind celebrating my freakish achievement."

She pushes me fondly. "You *are* a freak. You worry about the weirdest things."

Trista and Hank are busy trying to occupy the same space on a bench in the courtyard. Even the teacher on morning duty out here ignores them. They don't bother to pull apart as we approach.

"Who wants to go to Moonlight Madness this Saturday?" Natalie asks.

Caleb shrugs. I want to stab him in the neck.

Trista withdraws her tongue from Hank's mouth. "Is it time to celebrate?" she asks. "Finally? Hell yes, girl!"

"Hell yes!" Hank echoes. "Wait, what are we celebrating?"

"Andria is getting her license!"

And my stomach folds in on itself, like a tiny black hole. She is jinxing me, ruining everything. Something terrible is going to happen. Just like last time. Suddenly I feel cold and hot at the same time.

"Are you all right?" Alex asks, as he appears within my narrowing field of vision. He puts his hands on my arms. "You've just gone white as a ghost."

Gravity swallows me, and I am falling, falling, even though strong arms are holding me. And I can't escape this feeling that everything is ruined.

"Andria. Look at me and breathe."

Blue eyes. I focus on the eyes that hold my gaze, and I try to think about breathing. Why is it so hard?

"Andria!" Alex's fingers dig into my arms.

"Is she having a seizure?" I hear Trista ask.

No. Nonononono. God, no.

"That's right. Breathe with me." His blue eyes float in front of me. Beautiful blue. "Breathe."

His voice is low and steady, calming me. I feel my chest rise and my lungs fill with air.

Finally. I realize my heart has been thumping wildly this whole time, because now it's beginning to slow back to normal. My breathing is hard and fast too, but I don't want it to slow down. I can't slow it down. I want to keep the oxygen flooding my lungs. I feel desperate. Starving for air.

Alex's hands are cupping my face now. He stares at me with those angel eyes, and I think *oh, he's going to kiss me.* "Sweetheart, you have to breathe with me. You can do this."

Why won't he kiss me?

"You're going to be fine. Breathe with me. Slower."

But when I try to breathe slower, my chest trembles and I get frightened all over again.

Hypoxia is what caused me to have seizures when I was born. The thought of having a seizure here in front of everyone, in front of Alex, sends me into a new spell of panic. I'm going to seize. I've jinxed myself, and now I'm going to have a seizure.

Alex's hands are still holding my head, gently. "Come on. Breathe with me. Let me do the work for you. Inhale. Exhale. We'll do it together."

I pray to God and all the munchkins in Oz that I don't seize. That my limbs don't flail and my eyes don't roll back in my head. That I don't drool or pee on myself.

"Andria." His blue eyes are all I see. And I try really, really hard to concentrate. And I take one slow breath. His eyes widen, and he smiles at me. "Good."

I breathe with him again, and am suddenly aware of the cold sweat dripping down the back of my shirt. Ick. The rest of our immediate environment comes back into focus. The group of people that have probably been standing here all this time. The school nurse running over to us with Caleb.

"Bring her inside!" she says after taking one look at me.

Alex swings me up in his arms and follows the nurse back to her office. I feel gross now, and drained. Not as sleepy as I get when I do have a seizure, but I feel a similar sense of disorientation. I have to feel my way back into my body and the world around it.

He sets me down in the nurse's office on her faux leather couch. I've lain on this couch many times.

She brings me a cold wet washcloth so I can clean my face. "I'll take it from here, Alex," she says. "You and your friends need to get to class."

I want him to stay, but I also want him to leave. If I'm going to die of embarrassment, I'd rather do it without any more of an audience. "It's okay, I'll be fine," I say, holding the washcloth over my eyes so I can't look at his face.

"Okay." I hear the door open and shut. And then silence.

I should have told him thank you.

"Andria, do you want to call your mother?" the nurse asks.

I pull the cloth down from my face. "No, I think I'll be fine. It wasn't a seizure."

"Tell me what happened."

I describe the feeling of not being able to get enough air, the narrowing of my vision, the racing of my heart.

The nurse frowns. "Sounds like a panic attack. Has it ever happened before?"

I shake my head. "I'm not sure what I was panicking about."

"You're under a lot of stress, honey. With your stepdad in the news. And the loss of your sister is still pretty fresh. Did you ever talk to your mom about seeing a therapist?"

"No." I wonder how much the staff here discusses students. Has she been talking about me with Verla? "I'm fine, really. Maybe I just got a little overheated. Or dehydrated."

She doesn't say anything else. I hand her the washcloth, and she writes out a pass for me. I realize that all of my teachers must know that I'm the sexual predator's stepdaughter and they must all assume that I've been abused. That I'm damaged physically and emotionally. That I'm probably on the edge of sanity.

Dear God, my friends must think the same thing too.

I feel sick again. Wobbly. Shaky.

Oh no. My vision darkens and my ears start ringing and there's an awful metallic taste in my mouth.

Goddammit, no. I've jinxed myself after all. I tense up, knowing what's about to happen next.

"I think I want to call my mother after all."

At least I think that's what I say. The words might not actually make it out of my mouth, for the next thing I know I've slid from the sofa to the floor, and my head hurts.

"Andria!" The nurse is shaking me gently. "Are you all right?"

She helps me back up to the sofa. I blink at her, my whole body sore. I'm frightened at what's happening to me. I feel out of control. My body has betrayed me again. "I want to go home," I whisper, hoping the nurse can't hear my voice cracking.

"Your mother is coming," she says. "She's on her way now."

She is going to be even more overprotective after this, and I will never get my driver's license. I'm too tired to be angry anymore. Too tired to cry, even though I can feel the tears leaking out. Six months wasted.

Dammit.

"That was a pretty nasty seizure, Andria. It lasted almost five minutes. I know how you hate the Diastat, but I was worried I'd have to give it to you."

"No, there should be an order in my chart for Ativan. Mom said she talked to the doctor about it." I'd rather have a shot in my arm than a cold gel shoved up my butt.

"You're right," she says, flipping through the pages in the folder she's holding. "Good thing we didn't need it, though."

I lie down, my head on the arm of the sofa, until my neck begins to hurt. And even then I don't move.

I hate my life.

I must have drifted off because now my mom is here, signing me out and picking up my book bag. "Andria? Let's go, honey."

I sit up, stiff and wild-eyed. I don't know how long I've been sleeping. I feel only a little bit light-headed as I stand up and follow her out of the nurse's office. We leave school, and I have to blink for a moment in the bright afternoon sun.

"What time is it?" I ask.

"After two. I've called your doctor and he said we should go to the ER and have you looked at."

"No, please. I feel better already."

"Andria, you scared the hell out of that nurse. She says she's never seen a seizure last that long."

"I'm fine."

"No, you're not." Her voice rises, just enough, and I know I won't get any further arguing.

I get into the car, defeated. I'm silent as she drives across town to Athens Memorial. She pulls into the ER entrance. "I can walk just fine," I say. "Go ahead and find a parking space."

She finally relents, and at least I don't have to get into a wheel-chair to be taken inside. She signs me in, and the triage nurse takes my vitals. He's a nice older guy with a white moustache.

"Will you tell me what happened?" Mom asks, once we're taken to an exam room.

I climb up on the exam table and sigh. "I think it might have been a panic attack."

She frowns. "That's what the nurse said."

"I couldn't breathe." My legs swing off the side of the table. I make circles with my left then with my right foot. "And then I could, but I couldn't stop breathing fast. And then . . ." I hold up my hands. "And then I woke up on the floor and the nurse was threatening to give me Diastat."

"What was happening before that? Did something upset you?"

I shrug and concentrate on the foot circles.

"Honey, talk to me."

"We were talking about me getting my license. And going to Moonlight Madness to celebrate."

"And that upset you?"

I shrug again. "I think I just got overheated. Or maybe I didn't eat enough breakfast this morning."

The doctor comes in before Mom can say anything else, and I have to explain my symptoms one more time. He looks in my eyes, my ears, my throat. He listens to my chest and presses against my belly.

"In the computer it says you have a history of seizures, Andria. What medicines are you currently taking?"

"Lamictal and Phenobarbital."

He's looking in the computer to confirm this. "Any recent dosage change?"

"Her last checkup," Mom says. "Six months ago."

"Let's run a few tests and see if her medicine levels are still therapeutic. I'll also check to see if she's anemic. She looks a little pale."

"We don't eat a lot of red meat," Mom says.

The doctor types something into his computer and leaves.

Within a few minutes, a nurse comes in to draw blood. I've gotten used to needles over the years, but I still turn my head when she sticks me. "Do I get ice cream after this?" I ask Mom, wincing only a little. The nurse does a good job.

Mom rolls her eyes. "No ice cream."

I pull my phone out of my purse, and scroll through the numerous texts from Natalie and Trista. The text I'm looking for is not there. I put my phone back away.

But as we wait for the doctor to return with my lab results, I grow bored. I try lying back on the exam table, but it's uncomfortable and there's no pillow.

Mom has brought her tablet and is looking up healthy recipes on Pinterest. I pull my phone back out. Trista's last text asks,

So, are we still on for Saturday night?

Ugh.

We will definitely not be celebrating anything. I should be crying. I should be devastated. But I don't feel anything right now. Maybe the school nurse slipped me something after all.

Still nothing from Alex.

When the doctor finally comes back, he's smiling. "Everything looks fine. You just need to follow up with your neurologist."

"Her phenobarbital levels were normal?" Mom asks.

"Perfect. Continue taking your meds as prescribed and follow up with him in the next week or so. But come back and see us if your symptoms return."

Mom does not look happy with this nondiagnosis, but I slide off the table. "Can I go home?" I ask the doctor.

"Of course. Ask the lady at the front desk for a school excuse."

"I bet your friends were worried," Mom says as we walk out into the parking lot. An ambulance is pulling in, and we hurry to get out of its way.

"A little. They were excited about me getting my license."

"Weren't you excited too?" she asks as we get into her SUV. It's hot inside from the late-afternoon April sun beating down.

I throw my backpack on the floor between my feet and find the seat belt. "I was trying not to get my hopes up." And see, it was a good thing I didn't. And not just about driving. About Alex too. What is the point of having hope if it keeps getting taken away from you?

CHAPTER 24

Mom actually lets me stay home from school today, saying I need to rest up for tomorrow's doctor's appointment. She's still worried about my spell yesterday, even though I've told her a dozen times I'm fine.

I send Natalie a text, reassuring her I'm okay too, but just taking advantage of Mom's overprotectiveness. Then I roll back over and fall asleep.

When I wake up, I realize I need to write down yesterday's episode in my seizure journal. I shoved the black single-subject notebook on my bookshelf six months ago and haven't looked at it since. Right between the Harry Potter books and my *Backyard Astronomer's Guide*.

I didn't even have the heart to record the events the night Iris died. But I need to start keeping track again. I need to be a better patient and manage myself better. I grab a pen off my desk and sit back down on my bed to write. But when I open the notebook and look for a blank page, I find Iris's handwriting.

Sophie is whimpering at my bedroom door. I can hear Mom's raised voice coming from the kitchen.

★ ★ ★

Andria, you've gone with Mom to the hospital and I hope you're okay. It's my fault. I'm sorry I dragged you to Mike's tonight. I'm sorry I'm such a shitty sister. I'm a shitty daughter too, and I'm tired of disappointing people I love. I'm tired of not being brave like you. I've tried to be brave and stand up to Craig, but he says it will only hurt our family more if I say anything. There's no way I'll get out of this without pissing someone off. Without hurting you and Mom more than I already have. Without hurting Trista. I seriously fucked up tonight, and now I'm afraid I've lost her friendship. Alex deserves so much more than me. I can't be the light he needs. I hope he finds that light someday. I know what you did tonight, you did out of love for me. You sacrificed everything. I never deserved a sister as wonderful as you. I love you. PS. Sorry I took your pills, but I was kinda hoping the heroin would do the trick on its own. I have to make sure it works this time.

I touch the words on the page in horror, and I can hear my sister's voice in them. She deliberately killed herself. And she used my seizure journal to tell me good-bye.

I find Mom on the phone in the kitchen, her face white with anger. "No, I cannot accept that. This isn't right. He has to pay for what he's done."

I get a Diet Coke out of the fridge and let Sophie out into the backyard. I sit down at the bar, holding my journal and waiting for Mom to finish her phone call. I can tell it has to do with Craig. Something is wrong.

She slams her phone on the counter, and I'm amazed to see her shaking. I've never seen my mother not in control of herself. This makes me uneasy.

She is glaring but not at me. "He's accepted a plea bargain for a lesser charge. He won't go to jail and he won't be registered as a sex offender."

"Holy crap."

Mom is so pissed she doesn't say anything about my language. "I keep thinking of that poor girl and her family. She's been so brave, coming forward and talking with the detectives and he is still going to get away with what he did to her."

"Mom." I want to hug her, but she's pacing. She's vibrating with fury. "Mom," I try again, but my voice fades away. I don't know what else to say to her.

Sophie scratches on the kitchen door, and I let her back inside. She follows Mom as she paces into the living room. I follow both of them. My head hurts.

"Mom, you should read this." My hand is trembling as I hold out my journal. "All this time, it's been sitting on my shelf, and I never thought to look in it. I didn't need it . . ."

Mom reads the page, and I watch her eyes race over the words. She reads it again. She looks up at me, and I freeze.

She's crying.

I can't do anything but stare at her. She didn't cry when Iris died. I don't remember her crying when my father died.

She's crying now.

I am a horrible person. I have just broken my mother's heart.

She's picking her keys up from the end table, grabbing her purse. "I can stop him. I can lock him away. He has to pay for what he did to Iris."

Mom disappears into her bedroom. Sophie stays in the living room with me, huddled against me on the couch.

When my mother returns, she's holding Iris's diary and mine. I nod, aware of the pain she's about to put us both through. The trouble she could be in for not doing this earlier. She's going to turn them both in to the police.

It will be worth it, though. It's the right thing to do.

"Do you want me to go with you?" I ask. I scratch Sophie

between her ears, my contact with her giving me an anchor. Something normal to hold on to.

"No, you should try and get some rest," Mom says, coming forward and kissing me on the forehead. "The next few days will probably be exhausting."

But I can't sleep after she leaves. I think about school tomorrow. The community will blow up tomorrow when they hear the news. Just as the gossip was finally dying down after Craig's arrest.

Trista and Natalie will have to believe Kimber now. I hope Kimber can forgive my mom for not turning the diary over to the police initially. Mom was only trying to protect us.

It's too late to hide anymore.

Alex. He was Iris's boyfriend, and he deserves to know before they show Iris's diary on the six o'clock news. He shouldn't be blindsided with this news from strangers. He needs to know I can't blame him anymore for Iris's death. That I don't blame him.

It's only a little after twelve right now. Everyone should be out in the courtyard for lunch. I send him a quick text. *Come see me after school? We need to talk.*

He answers within a minute. *Can't. Sorry.*

I stare at my screen. At his words.

Can't. Sorry.

They don't change. Not even when I blink. What does he mean?

Are you mad at me? I text. Did my episode yesterday scare him away? He must have decided I am too much of a freak to love.

I'm broken, both physically and emotionally. Of course he should run as far away from me as he can.

He doesn't answer, and I wish I hadn't sent that last text. It sounds needy. God.

I should go ahead and get used to feeling this pain. There's no hope for us ever being together now.

By the time school's out, Mom is still not home and I'm tired of lying in bed trying to sleep. I get up and take a shower. I need to talk to Alex, and I need to get it over with.

Once he knows the truth, Alex is going to hate me, if he doesn't already.

CHAPTER 25

At his mother's suggestion, I find Alex at the AA meeting in the Lutheran church's fellowship hall. He's sitting in the front, head down and staring at the floor. I slip into the back because the meeting has already started and an older woman is standing up talking about her love for Oxycontin and Jack Daniel's. Back here, I can smell the fresh coffee and donuts waiting on the table.

At the break, I slide into the seat next to Alex.

He looks up and frowns at me. His eyes are red. "What are you doing here?"

"Your sponsor asked me to come to a meeting."

"Collin?" He doesn't believe me.

I fold my arms across my stomach, hugging myself. "He came to see me after school the other day. He's worried about you."

"Collin? Was worried about me?" Alex laughs, but it's bitter. "That asshole."

Shocked, I glance around the room, hoping his sponsor doesn't overhear him.

Alex's laugh dies away. "That's fucking great. Because he's the one that's in the ICU after OD'ing on Oxy last night."

I stare at Alex. The pain in his eyes kills me. "It's not your fault."

But for some reason, I can see he doesn't believe me.

"I'm so sorry," I whisper. I hate adding to his problems, but maybe I can actually relieve him of some of his guilt. "I came here tonight because we need to talk."

He glares at me. "I don't feel like talking. I don't want to end up hurting you too."

"No, please listen to me." I reach out for his arm, but he stands up, pushing the metal chair back. It almost tips over, but I catch it. And lose Alex.

He walks out of the meeting, and the African-American woman in charge of tonight's group sees us and starts toward me.

I pick my purse up off the floor.

"Are you a friend of Alex?" she asks.

I nod. "He said his sponsor slipped up."

"It wasn't Alex's fault," she says. "I know he doesn't believe that, but it's the truth."

"I met Collin a few days ago. He said he was worried about Alex."

I don't know how old this woman is, but she looks like she's been through hell and back. "I'm worried about Alex, too," she says. "But I'm not in danger of shooting up again. Collin was having problems of his own." She places a hand on my arm. I can see the old scars on the inside of her wrist. She looks strong and healthy now, a warrior. I'm jealous of the Zen aura she has about her. "I hope you can convince him to come back. I know he needs some time to mourn for Collin, but he shouldn't stay away so long again. We all miss him. I was so happy to see him here tonight, I hated telling him about Collin."

"I'll try," I say. But I have no idea what makes her think he'll listen to me.

Iris. That was the whole reason I came looking for him. He needs to know the truth about her death, now more than ever. I run out the door as the others help themselves to donuts.

He's not at the Indigo Dragon, so I tell his mom that I'll look at their house next. Kali rolls her eyes. "He quit AA again?" she asks. "All that money we wasted sending him to that holistic rehab in the mountains. Dammit."

His other mother, Sandra, nods her head, but her eyes are sad.

"You don't believe in him?" I ask both of them. "Why not?"

Sandra gives Kali a guilty look, and turns back to the kitchen.

Kali glares at me. I have no business telling them how to raise their son.

"I believe in him," I say. "And I want both of you to know that I don't blame him for Iris's death. It wasn't his fault."

Sandra returns from the kitchen with a takeout order for a customer.

Kali leans against the counter. There are tears in her eyes. "Really?" she asks. Her eyes are clear blue, just like Alex's. I want to hug her.

Instead I just nod. "And I don't want him to blame himself for something he's not responsible for. Alex is a good person. He deserves to be happy."

Kali's eyes open wide and her gaze falls behind me. "Alex?"

My cheeks go up in flames. I don't dare turn around, but I am suddenly aware how very close he is. Dammit.

"What the hell are you doing here?" he asks. His voice is angry, still hurting.

"I told you we need to talk."

"Why is my mom crying? Did you tell her about Collin? That I fucked up again?"

"What?" Kali asks.

"No!" Why does he give me such a headache? "Please just

listen to me." But I sound frustrated. And whiny. I hate when I sound whiny.

"Alex, go take Andria home," Kali says. "Then the three of us will talk tonight." She smiles at me, and I can see it makes Alex pause. "See you soon, Andria."

"Fine." He turns around to leave, and I kind of have to skip to make sure he doesn't leave me behind.

He doesn't say anything in the truck. This makes it easier for me. "Tomorrow, you're going to hear some news about Iris. And I wanted to tell you first so it doesn't shock you."

He stares straight ahead at the road.

And yes, I am feeling better. Thanks for asking, after yesterday's ER visit. I could say this out loud, but I always get into trouble with sarcasm. I take a deep breath.

"Mom and I found Iris's diary last week, and there was something terrible inside. We didn't want to tell anyone, but today I found a message she had written to me the night she died."

He turns into our neighborhood, his hands gripping the steering wheel.

"Please don't take me home yet," I say. "Mom is probably back from turning in the diary at the police station, and I need to tell you everything. Somewhere quiet."

He swallows, but doesn't look at me. "What did she write?"

It has to come out. I don't want to say the words, but he has to know. And once I say the words, I can't take them back. "Craig was abusing her. He'd been molesting her since she was twelve.

"That was the reason for all the drugs. She was trying to escape the pain." My hands twist in my lap. "And her overdose that night wasn't accidental. She left me a note saying good-bye."

His jaw clenches. "Why now? Why didn't you tell me as soon as you found the diary?"

"I wanted to," I say. "Mom wasn't going to turn the diary over to the police. She didn't want to drag Iris's name through the mud again. She didn't want anyone else to know. But Craig accepted a plea deal yesterday. He's about to be released from jail, with no further justice for Kimber. He's a monster. Mom went today and turned the diary over to the police, along with my seizure journal, which Iris had used to write a good-bye letter."

Alex pulls into his own driveway, in front of the garage. He turns off the engine and leans his forehead against his steering wheel.

"So, I wanted you to hear it. From me. I'm so sorry, Alex. Iris's death wasn't your fault."

The silence in the truck cab presses in on my ears. I grow self-conscious of my breathing. It becomes irregular.

"Are you saying," he says finally, "that Craig was abusing her even while we were dating?"

I think of her last diary entry, from almost a week before she died, and feel sick. "Yes."

He tears out of the truck and sprints into his house, leaving the front door open.

I wait for a moment before assuming that means it's okay to follow him inside. I finally go in, scared any minute I'm going to get yelled at.

But I hear him. I follow the sound to the hall bathroom, where he is retching so hard it makes my stomach hurt.

I go back and close the front door before he can see me. Then I find the kitchen to get him a glass of water. I give him privacy, but I can't leave him here alone.

My phone beeps, a text from Mom. I turn the ringer off and text her back, saying I'm with a friend and will be home before dark. I get one reply: *Be safe.*

I put the phone back in my purse when Alex comes out of the bathroom. I hold up the glass of water and a bottle of ibuprofen I found in the cabinet over the sink. I wasn't being nosy. I was looking for the glasses.

He takes the water but not the painkillers. "Thanks." He drinks it all and carefully sets the empty glass in the sink. He sits down at the table with me, and I feel some small relief. He's ready to talk.

"Exactly how long have you known?"

"Last week, when Craig was arrested, the police came to the house to ask questions. They asked me if he'd ever touched me. He never did, and I never had any reason to think he'd ever touched Iris."

"She never told you? Don't twins share their secrets? Don't you sense that kind of thing?"

I flinch at the anger in his voice. And then I blink back tears, because he's right. "I should have known somehow. But I didn't. I never imagined he was such a monster. The bastard would leave his sleep apnea machine running in the middle of the night so Mom wouldn't wake up and notice he wasn't sleeping. She never suspected anything either."

"Does Iris mention me in her diary?"

I nod. It would have been nice if Mom had let him read the diary before turning it over to the police. I don't know what to tell Alex. If I tell him the truth, it will sound like I'm trying to get him to forget about her. Should I lie and tell him she wrote about how much she loved him?

"No, forget it," he says, running his hand across his face. "I don't want to know."

I stare at him, wishing I knew the right thing to say.

He sighs. "Will you stay here while I take a quick shower? I feel really gross. Unclean."

"That will make you feel better," I say.

His laugh is short. Sarcastic. "If only. Will you stay?"

I nod.

I wait until I hear the sound of the water running and get up from the kitchen table to stretch. Their kitchen is beautiful and modern, despite being part of a hundred-year-old house. I walk down the hall and glance at the framed photos. Alex in various and assorted sizes. He had curly hair when he was little. Just like Kali.

The door to his bedroom is open and I peek inside. His walls are sky blue and bare. His bedspread a navy and black plaid. Other than a small pile of dirty clothes, his room is not as messy as I'd imagined a boy's room to be. A bass guitar is lying across the bed with an open notebook. The temptation to read it is strong, but I resist. What if he's been writing a song about Iris?

A library book sits open on his desk. Robert Frost. I sit down in the computer chair and wait. The room smells like cedar and sage and I recognize the woodsy scent I smell on him whenever we're close. I close my eyes and breathe in.

The water stops and the bathroom door opens. I panic. Didn't he take clean clothes in there with him?

Evidently not. I open my eyes to see him standing in the doorway, a towel slung low around his hips.

Alex stares at me, with water dripping from his shoulders. He is such a beautiful boy, I think. I feel a twinge in the bottom of my belly. Possibly in my ovaries. I need to look at something else besides his abs. Think about other things, Andria. Like baby pandas. Or cupcakes.

His cheeks turn pink. "What are you doing in here?"

I hop up from the chair. "Sorry, I thought you were getting dressed in the bathroom." As I scoot past him into the hallway, I catch the warm scent of shampoo and cedar.

I need to put more distance between us. Before I do something stupid.

He lets me pass, and I shut the door behind me. "I'll just wait in the kitchen," I say.

His voice is muffled. "No, stay right there."

As I stand in the hallway, I hear drawers opening and slamming shut. I hear wire hangers raking across a closet rod as they're shoved from side to side.

When he opens his door again, he's wearing jeans and a black T-shirt. "Please come sit back down. I . . . I think I'm ready to hear more." He gestures to his bed, and I give him a look.

He shrugs and spins his computer chair around for me like a gentleman.

I sit and roll it back closer to his bed, where he sits down. I place my hands in my lap, folding my fingers together like I'm about to say a prayer.

"I keep my own journal for my doctor. I record my seizures and write down each one's length, type, what was happening before, stuff like that. It helps him adjust my medication doses and helps me become more aware of my triggers. Like a severe lack of sleep."

Alex frowns and lies back on his bed, his hands behind his head.

"I hadn't written in my diary in over six months. Until I had the seizure yesterday. But it had been lying on my desk the night Iris died. She saw it and left me a message inside, while I was at the ER with Mom and Craig.

"But I never saw it. The morning she died I shoved the journal between some books on my bookshelf and forgot about it. Until this week when I pulled it out to record my last seizure."

I swallow the huge lump in my throat. I don't want to cry in front of Alex. "If I hadn't gone to the ER that night, Iris wouldn't have been left alone. And she wouldn't have taken my pills to add to the heroin and alcohol she had in her system. So really, it was my fault she died that night. Not yours."

He raises himself up off the bed on one arm. "You've got to

be kidding. It's not your fault. You had a seizure. You couldn't help it."

Dammit, he makes me cry. I wipe my face with the heel of my hand. He is going to hate me when I tell him everything that happened that night.

But it all has to come bubbling out. The ugly truth that I've kept locked inside for all these months.

"Alex. I faked that seizure."

CHAPTER 26

Six Months Ago

I really did have a seizure that night, but it had been way earlier in the evening. Iris had found me on the carpet in my bedroom, twitching and drooling, with Sophie pressed up against me, whimpering. Iris stayed on the floor with me until the seizure was over, and helped me up into my bed afterward. She brought a washcloth and stayed with me until the postseizure drowsiness started to wear off.

I was hysterical and told her not to tell anyone about the seizure. I was supposed to be taking the test for my driver's license the following Monday. If Mom knew, she'd tell my doctor and I wouldn't be able to take the test for at least another six months.

Iris didn't approve of me hiding something like that, but she knew how badly I wanted my license. And she promised to help me keep it secret. As long as I promised to go out with her that night and help with her cover story.

It was Saturday night, and we were supposed to be meeting Natalie and Trista at the mall. That's what we told Mom and Craig. Mall first, then going to eat at the diner out on Pembrook Street.

Instead, Iris drove us to a house somewhere on the other side of the university, just inside the Perimeter. I have no idea whose house it was or who was throwing the party, but that was the night Iris introduced me to Mike.

I'm sure it's not his real name, but I know he knew Iris and everyone else, calling them by their real names. Trista and Hank were there. We could hear them arguing in one of the back bedrooms. Mike grinned and said Iris would probably love to try the special blend he'd sold to Trista. Trista was already stoned out of her mind, he added, and Hank was desperately trying to catch up with her.

But Iris had other plans.

"You brought me here to babysit?" I demanded.

She shrugged. "Not really. I just wanted you to spend some time with us. Let loose a little, even if you can't party." But there was something in her eyes that I didn't like. An uneasiness. She was afraid of something.

"You don't have to do this," I whispered. "We can go home and bake cookies. They'll taste a hell of a lot better than whatever Mike's making in the kitchen."

She shook her head. "I don't want to go home. And you don't need to be cooped up there either. Come on, let's have some fun."

I glanced around the room at all the drugged zombies shuffling around. "This doesn't look like fun," I mumbled.

"Okay, fine. I need you to babysit then," she said. "Alex is already in the back room, and Mike's going to fix me up."

"I should call Mom," I say. "Or the cops."

She turned around, her eyes flashing. "And you'd be arrested right along with us. Do you want Mom to know about your seizure this afternoon? I'd hate for you to lose your driver's license before you even get it."

I glared right back at her. "You are evil."

She grinned and kissed me on the forehead. "You love me."

I was stupid not to stand up to her. I should have called the cops right then. Instead I followed her down the hallway into the back bedroom. It was empty, save for a few mattresses set out on the floor.

Alex was sitting on one of the mattresses, his back against the wall. His poufy rock-star bangs hung in his eyes, and he looked like an English sheepdog. "Ladies," he said, with a goofy smile. "Come fly with me."

I rolled my eyes, but Iris climbed over two unidentified bodies lying on the floor to reach him. The bodies rolled over and turned out to be Hank and Caleb, who were also, apparently, flying.

"Where's Trista?" I asked. "Is Natalie here too?"

"Went to get something to eat," Alex said, as Iris climbed into his lap. "In the kitchen."

I turned around and let them have some privacy. Hank and Caleb were too stoned to pay attention to them. But I didn't want to watch.

The kitchen was dingy, just like the rest of the house. Old vinyl flooring was curling up in places, and the fluorescent lighting hummed loudly. I was afraid it was going to explode at any minute.

Trista was not in the kitchen. Two girls wearing sorority shirts from the university were making what looked like Kool-Aid, making a mess on the counter. A guy with blond dreadlocks was pulling chocolate chip cookies out of the oven. They smelled so good, but I didn't dare eat anything in this house.

"Thirsty?" one of the sorority girls asked me.

I shook my head, wishing I'd brought my own Diet Coke with me. "No, thanks."

I texted Natalie, hoping she was somewhere in the house, but when she answered, it was to say she was at a cousin's birthday party with her family. Great. I had no backup that night.

This didn't seem to be the typical keg party that Iris and Trista usually liked to attend. There was no loud thumping music, and the front yard wasn't packed full of cars. It was rather low-key, as if whoever was throwing the party was going out of their way not to piss off the neighbors.

One of the rooms smelled like pot. I already knew what that smelled like. But the other room, with Alex and Iris, had a more sinister smell. Like butterscotch and vinegar.

Iris was still in the back bedroom with Alex. I was aware again of the absence of wall-thumping music, and realized most people in the room were getting their bliss on with their own private sound track, courtesy of earbuds.

Alex was sitting next to Iris, his eyes closed while he was off in his own world. Iris was smiling at something Mike was saying to her, as he handed her a piece of aluminum foil. He was showing her how to fold it and hold a cigarette lighter underneath.

Cold black fear slithered up inside me. I stumbled over someone's body as I tried to reach my sister. "Iris!"

She held what looked like a homemade cigarette to the foil and sucked in.

She had her earbuds in, but my shriek was loud enough for her to hear. Still, she had a hard time lifting her head and looking up at me.

I squatted down in front of her instead. "What are you doing?" I asked, panicking. "I thought you were smoking pot with Alex. What the hell is that?"

Her eyes rolled back. "Pot doesn't work," she murmured.

Mike put his things away in a black bag. It looked like an old fashioned doctor's bag. "Sweet dreams, Iris." He noticed me and did a cartoonish double take. "Whoa. Two Irises. Want to chase the dragon with her?"

"Stay away from me," I said.

"Whatever you say, Doppelgänger." He grinned and took his bag of poison across the room, where the dreadlocked boy from the kitchen was waiting for him. For him, Mike pulled out a tourniquet and a tiny syringe.

We shouldn't have been there, in that house. I should have called the cops and dragged Iris home no matter what she told Mom.

Instead, I went outside and sat on the front porch step, looking for stars. The woods behind those houses backed up against the city's enormous cemetery, so it was nice and dark. I sat outside for a long time, letting my eyes adjust to the darkness, but the sky was too cloudy. It might have been a bad omen.

Trista stumbled outside, her eyes wild and her cheeks burning red. "Are you okay?" I asked.

It took her a moment to focus on what I was saying. "No, I'm fine. Where's Hank?"

"In the back with Alex and Iris."

But she had already disappeared into the house.

I followed her back, but neither she nor Hank were there when I found Iris, leaned up against Alex. I glared at Mike, who had apparently finished medicating Dreadlocks.

"How long will her high last?" I asked him.

"A few hours. She's only smoked a few times, so it lasts longer for her than for some of these other guys."

"She's done this before?" I asked, horrified. What kind of person had my sister become? And why hadn't I noticed?

"Listen, if you're going to stay here with her, I need to make a phone call. Watch those two," he said, nodding to Iris and Alex. "Keep them upright and don't let them choke on their own puke."

I felt like gagging myself. I glared at my sister's boyfriend. And kicked him in the shin. "Did he get her started on this?" I asked Mike. But the drug dealer had already left.

Alex slid over on his side, but I ignored him. I didn't care if he choked or died. Instead, I bent down beside my sister.

"Iris." I pulled an earbud out of one ear. "Iris!"

She didn't open her eyes, but she smiled. "You're here. You're safe."

"We're not safe," I said, shaking her. "We need to get out of here."

"Noooo, I like it here. Everyone I love is here." She frowned for a moment, but then her face smoothed out. "I love you, Andria."

"I know." I wondered if I'd be able to carry her if it came down to it.

"Don't make me go home just yet. I like it here. In heaven."

Her eyes were still closed. I looked around the dim room full of drugged bodies. There was a clear path to the door. I pulled her earbud out again and held it up to my ear. She was listening to a Calcifer song. I recognized Thing One's voice singing about darkness and light. I leaned my head against her shoulder and closed my eyes for one moment. I tried to wait for her to come back to me. She smelled like sweat and pot and rancid butterscotch, but underneath all of that, I could also smell her favorite body lotion. Cherry blossoms.

No, I couldn't wait. We had to get out of there. I pulled the earbuds away. "Come on, Iris! It's time to go to school!"

Her eyes flew open. "Now?"

"Yes. Now. If we hurry we won't be late."

"Okay." She let me stand her up. But her face looked pale. "I don't feel good."

"That's fine," I said, leading her out of the room, away from Alex. "I'll drive."

"We'll get into trouble. You shouldn't be driving." Her eyebrows were scrunched up. She was trying to remember something important.

"It will be okay. We'll be sneaky."

The frown on her face turned into something more serious. Distress. She stopped walking. "I don't like being sneaky."

I grabbed her arm and tried to hurry her down the hallway. "Seriously? Then you shouldn't have been sneaking around and smoking heroin. Why would you do such a thing? Why couldn't you tell me?"

But Iris was silent as she allowed me to drag her out the door to the car.

"How long have you been doing hard stuff like this?" I asked, helping her into the front passenger seat.

She pouted, and her head lolled back. I could hear one of the sorority girls giggling from the front porch.

Then I remembered. Trista. I couldn't leave her at that house alone. Once I had Iris buckled in, I went back inside to find her best friend. I hoped that it would be easier to persuade her to leave.

But I found Trista straddling a drugged out Hank-Zombie, riding him like she was a jockey in the Kentucky Derby. "Tris!" I shouted, wishing that there was truly such a thing as brain bleach. "It's time to go home!"

She looked over her shoulder at me, her eyes perfectly clear and sober. "Don't worry about me. I'll make sure the boys make it home safe."

The stony look in her eye made me uncomfortable. No matter what drugs she'd taken earlier that night, she seemed fully aware of what she was doing. Even if Hank wasn't.

"Fuck, woman!" Hank shouted. He must have been aware after all.

I took one last look at the Alex-Zombie. He was still breathing.

Pity.

And he looked like he was starting to come down from his high. I wasn't going to waste any more time worrying about him.

"Call me when you've got them home," I told Trista. But I wasn't sure if she had my number or not. "Just call Iris's phone."

She rolled her eyes and never lost her rhythm.

When I got back to the car, Iris was beginning to come down. But her pupils were still tiny pinpoints. I dug through her purse for the keys.

"You're not supposed to drive," she said. "You're post-ictal. Ictal. Ictal." She became fascinated with the word describing my sleepy state after a seizure.

"It's fine," I said, starting the car. "I'm a safer driver than you right now."

As I drove carefully back across town, I tried to push the guilt out of my head. Stupid brain, betraying me when I needed it most to behave. I couldn't miss the driving test on Monday. I had to get my license.

Iris was still amusing herself. "Ictal. Ichthyologist. Ichabod Crane."

Hopefully she wouldn't even remember my seizure in the morning.

"I kept you safe, didn't I?" she asked me suddenly.

I nodded. "We're both safe," I said, pulling into our neighborhood. "I keep you safe too."

She let out a sob. "You can't. It's too late for me."

Iris dozed off until I pulled into our driveway, right behind Mom's and Craig's cars. It wasn't quite midnight, so I was afraid they would still be awake. I hoped I could get Iris to her room to sleep before they saw us.

"Iris, look at me." I turned the map light on overhead.

"Shit! What was that for?"

"Crap, your pupils are still effed up. If you can't walk straight, we'll both be grounded."

She giggled at me, and then noticed the cars in the driveway. She started to cry.

"Just be quiet," I said as we got out of the car.

As soon as she slammed her door shut, the porch light came on.

"Oh shit," she muttered.

I thought about all the trouble Iris would be in if they found her. I thought about how I had begged her to lie for me and help keep me out of trouble.

"When we get inside," I told her, "don't pay any attention to me. Just go straight to your room and go to bed."

Before she could argue, the front door opened and Mom stood in the foyer. "There are my girls! You're both home earlier than we expected."

"I wasn't feeling good," I said, pretending to lean on Iris even though I was really holding her up. I hoped Mom wouldn't get a good look at her.

It didn't work.

"What's wrong with Iris?" she asked, trying to pull us apart.

I fell to the floor in the foyer. I had no idea what my seizures looked like, even though I'd asked Iris once to record me having one, out of morbid curiosity.

She never did. I jerked a little, ignoring the pain I felt from hitting the cold hard floor. I tried to drool a little, and I let my eyes roll back as far as I could, but it gave me a headache.

Mom cried out for Craig and dropped to the floor beside me.

I knew the doctor had once told Mom to take me to the ER if a seizure ever lasted longer than five minutes. But I had no idea how long I needed to lie there and twitch. I could feel Mom patting my shoulder, smoothing my hair.

Craig loomed over me, his hands in his pockets. I could hear the change jingling as he fidgeted. I didn't hear Iris. I prayed it was because she'd done as I asked and gone straight to bed.

"Craig, it's not stopping," Mom said. Her voice was anxious.

"Should we call an ambulance?" he asked. I could smell his aftershave and had to fight not to gag.

"I don't know," Mom said. "How long do you think it's been?"

I kept up the twitching, even though my arms and legs were getting tired. I didn't want Mom to leave and check on Iris just yet.

"Oh, sweetheart," Mom crooned. "And you were about to take your driving test on Monday. I'm so sorry."

I ignored the disappointment smothering the air in my chest. Really. I had had a seizure. I didn't deserve to get a license anyway. Obviously my epilepsy was not very well controlled, and it would have been irresponsible of me to get a license when it was unsafe for me to drive.

I kept telling myself these things over and over, but it didn't make it hurt less.

"I'm calling 911," Craig said. "Do you think she forgot to take her medicine?"

"I don't know," Mom snapped. "I'll be sure to ask her when she comes to."

They didn't fight often, but when they did, it was because of their differing views on parenting. Craig always thought Mom should have let me play soccer. But she balked and finally had him convinced I would be a sickly invalid the rest of my days.

I had to work extra hard not to smile at Mom's irritation. I was growing so tired I was worried I was going to throw myself into another real seizure. I slowed the twitching once I heard the paramedics arrive. I finished my performance with only a few occasional last jerks.

"Andria?" Mom hovered close over me. "Honey?"

Slowly, I opened my eyes. I looked at Mom and blinked.

"I'm so sorry, baby."

I curled over on my side and started to sob. "No!" It didn't take much theatrics. The tears were real. I really had just crushed my own hopes and dreams.

The paramedics examined me and discussed my medical history with Mom. They convinced her that I should go ahead to the ER and be checked out by a physician. I felt guilty when I thought of the hospital bill Mom and Craig would be receiving for this.

Mom rode with me in the back of the ambulance, where the swaying motion made me nauseated. I closed my eyes and tried to sleep, but it was impossible and the ride was thankfully a short one.

I had been ten the last time I went to the ER for a seizure. That one had lasted twenty minutes, and my lips had turned blue. I've heard that people who are depressed can be shocked by doctors, who purposely cause seizures in an effort to cure their depression. I can't imagine going through these painful storms willingly. I worried about my brain being permanently scrambled from each one.

The ER doctor on duty that night was an older Asian woman. She shined a light in my eyes and ordered blood work and a urine test. She must have smelled the pot on me.

My body was drug-free except for my antiseizure medication. My phenobarbital level was within normal therapeutic levels. My oxygen level was fine.

"Did she hit her head?" the doctor asked my mother.

I realized that I might have when I'd had the real seizure earlier, and reached up to touch the back of my skull. When I winced, the doctor ran her gloved fingers across my scalp and ordered a CT.

It was negative. No concussions, no intracranial hemorrhage, no swelling.

It was almost three o'clock in the morning when we finally left the ER. Craig had arrived an hour and a half after we did, with Mom's car. I fell asleep in the backseat as they took me home.

"Don't forget to write this episode down in your journal," Mom said as I dragged myself to my room.

I wanted to cry all over again. Six more months. I didn't want to think about the stupid journal. Why would I write down a fake seizure anyway? The journal was sitting open on my desk like it usually was, but I shoved it between two astronomy books on the highest bookshelf. I wanted to forget all about my epilepsy.

I prayed my sister would wake up later that morning sober and that we could have a serious discussion about her life choices. I changed into my pajamas and barely stayed awake long enough to brush my teeth before tumbling into bed. I think it was almost four by that time.

I woke up a few hours later to Mom's screaming. "Iris! Iris! Wake up! Craig! Call 911 again!"

I jumped out of bed, racing to my sister's room.

Iris was pale, cold and still.

No. No. No. No. No.

Mom tried giving rescue breaths and began pumping on Iris's chest. She'd kept up her CPR training because of me. I'm sure she never thought she'd be using it on Iris.

She was still pumping and breathing and pumping and breathing when the paramedics arrived and took over. They looked grim but continued to attempt bringing my sister back.

Then there were two policemen there, and the paramedics stopped CPR.

"What are you doing? She needs to go to the hospital!" Mom cried. Craig put one arm around her and the other around me.

I shrugged him off and reached for Iris's hand.

It was so cold.

This was a nightmare, and I was certain I was going to wake up at any minute. But Mom pulled me away from Iris, and I didn't wake up.

They zipped my sister up in a big black bag that reminded me of Mike's little black bag of poison, and I still didn't wake up.

They wheeled her out the front door, and the police asked me questions about the previous night. I still didn't wake up. I told them we were at a party, and I thought my sister was drinking. I thought I smelled pot, and I had talked Iris into coming home.

"Were you drinking too?" the police asked.

"No, I take seizure medicine," I answered.

"She had a seizure last night after they came home," Mom said. "We took her to the ER."

"The victim?" one of the police asked.

"No. Andria," she said, pointing to me.

"Do you know the name of the person throwing last night's party?" the police asked. "Whose house was it?"

I shrugged. "Someone Iris knew. Over near the college." It

didn't matter anymore. I couldn't protect her any longer. So why should I protect the rest of them?

"Her boyfriend, Alex Hammond, was there," a vicious little imp inside me said. "Maybe he knows whose party it was."

The police scribbled his name down in their file. "We'll be sure to talk to him then. Thank you, Andria. Mr. and Mrs. Williams, sorry for your loss."

CHAPTER 27

"I'm so tired," Iris had written in that message to me. *"There's no way I'll get out of this without pissing someone off."* Without hurting anyone.

The death certificate states my sister died from asphyxiation, lack of oxygen secondary to consumption of heroin.

But Iris surprised us. The toxicology report confirmed that she did have alcohol and heroin in her system, but she also had phenobarbital. One of my medications.

She was alive when I left in the ambulance with Mom. Craig stayed behind, possibly to sneak into her room and take advantage of her drugged state. Sometime after Craig drove to the hospital, Iris wrote in my journal, telling me good-bye. She probably thought I'd see it the next day. She still had enough alcohol and heroin in her system that when she took my phenobarbital, her body forgot how to breathe.

The coroner estimated her time of death between three and four. If I hadn't faked the seizure, I would have still been at the house and maybe that monster wouldn't have gone into her room. If I'd only gone to check on her before I went to sleep.

Three hours earlier, Mom's CPR might have succeeded.

My sister's death was my fault.

Alex looks up at me, his eyes red and bright. "You can't know that. If Craig had been in her room many times before without you waking up, what makes you think you would have heard that night? Even if you'd been there to stop her from taking the pills, even if you'd prevented Craig from going in her bedroom, it would have only saved her for one night."

He stands up and starts to pace. "Dammit, why couldn't she have told me about him? Did she think I was that fucked-up that I couldn't help her? I guess she was right."

"No," I say, standing up too. I want to move closer to him, but I stop. I don't think I can comfort him right now.

I swallow the bile in my throat. One more truth that he needs to hear. "It was the opposite, Alex. She wrote that she couldn't be the light you needed. She thought she was too effed up to help you."

He's quiet. So quiet I can hear the heater turn on, hear the warm air blow through the vent in his ceiling.

"I'm sorry I narced on you that day, and gave the police your name."

When the police went to talk to Alex, his moms made him take a home drug test and promptly shipped him off to rehab. He wasn't even able to attend Iris's funeral.

Not that my family would have been happy to see him there.

"Telling the cops about me probably saved my life," he says. "Thank you."

I shrug. "I didn't think I was doing you a favor at the time, but I'm glad it worked out."

"I'm sorry," he says, finally. His voice is tired. Defeated.

The despair I've been feeling turns to anger. I find myself pushing him in the chest in fury. "Stop saying that!" I say. "You're always apologizing! I'm sick of it. You don't have any reason to apologize. Yes, I know I blamed you for Iris's death for a long time. But I didn't know about Craig. And I didn't know she'd taken my pills and I didn't know she'd written a good-bye note."

I calm down, and place my hands on his heart. I feel it pounding beneath my fingertips. "I'm sorry, Alex. Please, please don't blame yourself anymore. I hope you find the light you need."

I leave his room, then his house. I'm exhausted. Drained. But I walk home without looking back.

I half want him to run after me, to confess that I, Andria, am the light he needs. The light to chase away his darkness. And the heavens will shine down and we'll kiss like a happy couple at the end of a Shakespearean comedy.

But I know it won't happen. This is Greek tragedy. And I'm just as broken as he is.

CHAPTER 28

I've made peace with the fact that I'm not going to see my driver's license before I'm thirty. It's out of my control, really. I've accepted that.

My grades are something I do have control over, though. With Verla's extra credit and me putting more effort into my homework, my English and algebra grades could both jump to high Bs by the end of the semester. I can live with Bs. I can still end my junior year on the honor roll.

Trista and Natalie are upset about the seizure, but still want to take me to Moonlight Madness miniature golf this weekend.

Even when Iris's diary goes public. Even when the neighbors turn nasty and Mom loses her position as president of the homeowner's association. Natalie offers to bring enough food and toilet paper for my mom and me so we never have to leave the house. It's not like reporters and TV crews are camped out in the front yard, but they have been calling relentlessly. Mom got the house phone changed, along with both of our cell numbers. She vetoes the miniature golf outing but lets the girls hide out here with me instead.

She's kept me home from school the rest of this week, worrying that stress caused last week's seizure. It's Friday night, and we're all hanging out in the living room, which Trista lovingly calls the Bunker. It does feel like we're under attack.

Even Natalie asks if Craig molested me. I know the rest of Athens must be assuming the same thing. I tell the girls Craig must have been turned off by my epilepsy because no, he never touched me.

Trista laughs until Natalie hits her in the arm.

I shouldn't mind what people think. It was terrible what my sister went through, and a part of me feels guilty that I didn't go through it with her. Survivor's guilt, Mom said it's called. She is starting to think I do need to see a counselor. She actually made an appointment for me and is thinking about seeing one herself.

I think of Ismene, wanting to share the blame with Antigone for her brother's burial, and Antigone rejecting her. Iris thought she was protecting me all those years, by not sharing her secret with me. By suffering in silence.

As sick as it sounds, I would gladly have shared her burden if it meant I wouldn't have had to lose her.

Mom's attorney says he's hoping Craig will confess when he is shown the diary. That he will be given a minimum jail sentence of ten years and will have to register as a sex offender. Georgia laws are strict. When he does get out of jail, he won't be able to live within a thousand feet of any place where children congregate.

I think about Kimber, and how angry she must be at Iris. If Iris had told someone earlier, if Craig had been arrested a long time ago, would Kimber have been safe?

What if there were girls before Iris? Craig was a soccer coach long before he married Mom. They met when Iris first started playing in elementary school, and Craig was helping out with her team.

I feel sick thinking about him. I feel sick thinking about what my sister went through.

Natalie has brought cupcakes over that her mom made. Carrot cake with cream cheese frosting. Trista brought crab rangoons from Jade Palace, where she just started working. Just for one night, we pile on the couch together and watch silly Japanese anime and try to forget how terrible the world is.

Boys are not discussed. Caleb was arrested yesterday for trying to sell weed to an undercover cop. It doesn't look like Hank had anything to do with it, but he is conveniently visiting an uncle in Florida. No one talks about Alex. And I have not heard from him all week.

I try not to think about him. It's easy right now, surrounded by people and distracted with colorful characters to watch on television.

But at night, when everyone crashes in my room, I curl up wide awake in my futon chair, with Sophie sleeping underneath. Natalie is already snoring on her air mattress, and Trista is tossing and trying noisily to get comfortable on my bed. I stare out the window, where dim half moonlight has lit up the backyard and the trees beyond.

I can't help but wonder if Alex is having trouble sleeping. If he's still having nightmares in his room not far behind those woods.

"Hey." Trista's voice is barely a whisper.

I glance toward the dark corner of the bedroom, where my bed is. I can make out Trista, curled up on her side, staring at me.

"Did Iris say anything about me in her diary? Or . . . in the note she wrote to you?"

I wish I could have copies printed up and distributed. We could have a book club meeting at the library to discuss.

But I feel like a bitch for thinking this. Trista was Iris's best friend. She probably never suspected anything either. She's feeling just as betrayed and guilty as I am. "She worried that she'd fucked up and that you were mad at her."

Trista rolls over on her back and stares at the ceiling. "Shit."

Natalie rolls over on the air mattress, and even with the soft bedding Mom gave her, it still squeaks and makes a lot of noise. But Natalie doesn't wake up. She snores on, just like Sophie.

"What happened?"

Trista sighs. Or sobs. I can't tell in the dark, but I think she's crying. "That night at the party, she kissed me."

I don't know what I was expecting, but it certainly wasn't this. Maybe that Iris had kissed Hank? I'm not sure what to say. "Why?" is all that comes to mind.

Trista laughs. "Beats the shit out of me. I thought she was just stoned or drunk. I didn't know about the heroin until the next day. I mean, I don't know if that made any difference or not. I pushed her away and she looked so hurt. Like she'd been having feelings like that about me for a long time."

She rolls back onto her side, to look at me. "But I didn't. And I don't think I ever gave her the impression that I did. But now you're telling us her death wasn't an accident and I can't help but wonder if it was because of me. Alex wasn't giving her what she needed, but what if she thought I could? And I couldn't? Didn't?"

I should have told Trista she didn't have to tell me about this. That whatever Iris did or said to her should have stayed a secret between them. But I'm glad she could talk to someone.

"Maybe we all failed her," I say finally. "Because we didn't know she needed help."

"I know, but . . . shit. I didn't love her that way, but she was my best friend. I should have been more supportive."

I remember that night, seeing Trista screwing Hank like her life depended on it, and it sort of makes sense to me now. She was trying to convince herself of something.

"Do you love Hank?" I ask.

"Honestly? Yes. I know we act like a pair of bickering five-year-olds sometimes, but yeah, we do love each other. We've been talking about leaving together after high school. Getting out of this town."

"College?" I ask. Somehow, I didn't think Hank had the GPA or the temperament for that.

"He wants to join the air force, like his dad. I could go to junior college just about anywhere."

"What do you want to study?"

"Something medical, but not nursing. I peeked at my sister's books. I don't think I'd be interested in that. Maybe radiology? Taking pictures of people's bones all day sounds like it would be cool."

I imagine grown-up Hank and Trista, doing grown-up things like being in the military and working at a hospital. It makes me smile.

"Hank would have to get rid of his green Mohawk."

She shrugs. "He looks sexy bald too."

"Oh dear Lord," I say.

"What about you?" Trista asks. "Iris said you wanted to study astronomy? I saw that huge telescope out on the back deck."

"Yes. But the universities have even bigger ones."

"Bigger is not always better, darling. Take Hank, for example."

"No!" I whisper, trying hard not to laugh and wake up Natalie. "I don't want to hear this!"

Trista grins. "Fine. Then, can we talk about you and Alex?"

My good mood disappears. Trista is relentless in her girl bonding tonight. "There's nothing going on between us."

"You might fool yourselves, but neither of you are fooling the rest of us. Even Hank notices the chemistry between you guys. I know it's got to be weird. But I think it's also right."

Weird, I get. "How could you possibly see us as right for

each other? He dated my twin. He'll expect me to replace her. Or I'll worry that he's constantly comparing me to her."

"I think losing Iris ties the two of you together. You can help each other move on. Move forward."

I'm silent for a while. "You lost her too," I say finally. "And I think your grief is tangled up with ours as well. So why not you and Alex?"

"But I have Hank. And he's been there for me all these months. Who did you have? Who did Alex have?"

I can't stand it when someone else is more logical than I am.

"Maybe one day," I say. But I worry about Mom's recent wish to move. Is she serious? What if she decides she absolutely can't live here anymore and wants to start over before my senior year?

I hear Trista settling back against my pillows. "Are you sure you'll be comfortable in that chair?" she asks.

"I'll be fine. Don't worry. I'm not going to sneak into bed with you to snuggle after you've gone to sleep."

It's not a funny thing to say in this house, though. Even if Trista knows I'm saying it to be funny.

"Good-night, Andria."

"'Night," I say. And my futon is comfortable. I've slept in it many times before. But my head is full of racing thoughts. Alex. Iris. Trista.

When I hear Trista's breathing slow down and become regular, I get out of the chair and sneak out to the kitchen. The microwave clock says it's only two thirty. Too early to expect to see Alex jogging, but then again, I haven't seen him running in over a week.

Mom has donated Craig's sleep apnea machine to a local charity clinic, and has replaced it with a traditional noise machine. I hear ocean waves and whale songs coming from her bedroom.

Quietly, I unlock the back door and step out onto the patio. And am shocked by how cold it is outside. And windy. A cold front is settling in. I look up and smile when I see a clear black sky full of stars.

It's already April; we shouldn't be having cold fronts anymore. Not like this. I hop up and down in my bare feet, my toes getting numb. But I want to look through my telescope for one thing. The asteroid Iris. I do not have any objects in space that share my name. I hope to change that one day. But Iris has two. An asteroid and a meteor. Neither one is close to Earth, but I did find a photo of her meteor in a copy of *Astrophotography Magazine* once.

Iris seemed excited when I showed her. But she asked me to name a nebula after her if I ever discovered one. That was when she stole my nebula ring because she thought it was pretty.

I still want to discover Asteroid Andria one day. Or Comet Andria. But I promised my sister, one day I would find the Iris Nebula.

I point my telescope toward the northeast, where Sagittarius and Hercules are hanging out. This time of the year, it's possible to catch a glimpse of Iris's asteroid, even though it's very faint and part of the belt between Mars's and Jupiter's orbits.

I am freezing, but I don't want to go back inside to get warmer clothes. I don't want anyone to wake up and join me. I'll thaw out my toes later. The heavens are waiting for me right now.

With my strongest-powered lens, I find the asteroid belt, and can pick out some of the larger inhabitants. Ceres. Juno. But there's only so far I can see with the equipment I have. I feel like I'm blind when I try looking out into the universe. Nearsighted.

I want to see farther. I want to know what else is out there.

I want to see what's coming next.

But there's no way to see that. And there's no way I'm able

to see Asteroid Iris even with my new lens from Alex. I put the cover over the telescope and go back inside. But instead of returning to my room, I slip into Iris's bedroom and lie down on her bed.

It doesn't smell like her anymore. Mom has washed the bedding more than once, but she keeps putting off packing things away. She knew I liked to come in here often, before I knew about our stepfather.

This bed should probably be burned after the things Craig did in here. Now, I feel like an intruder, surrounded by pain and fear. And yet I remain. Because I couldn't be here for her when she was alive.

Iris, I'm here now. And I miss you so much.

CHAPTER 29

I dream of Iris. She's back in that dead forest, with the damp brown leaves covering the forest floor. She is walking away from me now through the trees. Into the shadows.

I try to follow her, but the forest grows thicker and fills with mist. She's moving farther and farther away. I hear a high-pitched buzzing in my ears, but can't find the source of the sound anywhere. I run farther into the forest toward the shadows, but my sister is gone.

I wake up drenched in sweat, disoriented. My heart is racing. The buzzing present, but fading away. It takes me a moment to remember where I am. In Iris's bedroom. I drag myself out of her bed and stumble to the bathroom to wash my face. The cold water wakes me up. The last of the dream is scrubbed away.

The girls leave late in the morning after Mom makes us whole-grain waffles with strawberries and whipped cream. Natalie leaves the remaining cupcakes. "Take one a day as needed. With Diet Coke. Repeat in six hours if no results."

I roll my eyes. "What results?"

"Mom says cupcakes are the cure for unhappiness."

I hug my best friend. "Tell your mom thank you. She is a wise woman. And a kick-ass baker."

Trista hugs me too. "Hope things start to settle down soon. Are you going back to school Monday?"

"I think so." I hope so. This week has dragged on forever.

The house grows quiet again after my friends leave. Mom, who's been getting as stir-crazy as me, decides we are going to brave the city and get some fresh air. She drags me out for lunch at the Mediterranean restaurant downtown.

"It was good to see you having fun with your friends," she says, once we're settled at a table on the back deck. It's a little chilly, but we're bundled up warmly and the sun is shining. We share a plate of hummus and warm pita bread while we wait for our lunch.

"Thanks for letting me have them over."

She squints at me, shading her eyes with her hand. "Andria, I still want to move. I don't think I can stay in our house anymore."

"You want to move now? Before I finish school?"

"I'm sorry. But I think you might do better in a new environment. With new people."

"That don't know our family."

She doesn't have to answer. I see the relief on her face that I understand. She wants to put all of this behind us.

"I don't want to hide anymore, but I don't want to leave Athens," I say. "We shouldn't have to."

"Honey, I know that. But everyone knows now what happened. How do you think my employer is going to treat me? My clients? What about your teachers and the other students?"

Mom's job depends on her popularity, in a way. Athens's Top Real Estate Agent of 2014 and 2015 can't have an ex-husband who's a convicted sex offender.

"It hasn't been bad for me." The hummus doesn't taste quite so yummy anymore.

She sighs. "I've had an offer of a position in Atlanta."

"As a real estate agent?"

"I'd be property manager for a commercial office building, leasing out office space in the downtown area. Not really the same thing I've been used to, but I think I'd like to try something different."

She's been planning to move all along. Even though she said she'd wait. She really wants to start over and forget everything about her life in Athens. Forget about Iris and everything that happened to her.

I tear a piece of pita bread in half and then in half again. "Did you already accept?"

"No. But I really want to, Andria."

She's going to make me feel guilty about wanting to stay. I lose my appetite, even though I have a plate of chicken shawarma coming.

"I really think it's for the best."

"I'd have to make new friends and explain my seizures all over again. And find a new doctor. And learn to drive in Atlanta." All of these things terrify me.

The waitress brings our lunch platters and refills our drinks.

I wonder about the process of getting emancipated. I wonder what kind of job I could get that would allow me to remain in Athens.

"We could get a place with a pool. You've always said you wanted a pool."

She's desperate, I realize. She has always been terrified of me swimming and having a seizure. "I don't want a pool. I want to stay here." I don't know if throwing a tantrum is the best tactic for me to take, but I'm so close to tears, I'm afraid I'll start pounding and kicking the floor next. I hate her for waiting until we were out in public to spring this news on me.

Mom sighs, pushing her food around on her plate. "What if we went somewhere totally different? California? England? Australia?"

I blink. "Are you serious? You want to yank me out of Athens that badly?"

"What's keeping you here?" she asks.

Alex. "My life is here. Your life is here."

"I don't want us to have this life anymore," she says.

When the waitress comes back to check on us, I ask for a box. I can't eat now. I'm too upset.

Mom is silent, her lips pressed tightly together in a thin line, but nods when the waitress asks if we're ready for the check.

Neither one of us speaks the whole ride home. She's unhappy that I'm unhappy, but she's still going to go through with it anyway. She's made up her mind that this is the best thing to do. There's no way I can talk her out of it.

We pull into the driveway, and Alex is sitting on our front porch step.

Mom is not happy. Her hands grip the steering wheel. "Why is he here?"

"Not sure, but I would like to talk to him." *I will talk to him, whether you like it or not.*

"Andria, he was a bad influence on Iris. I don't want him getting your head messed up too."

I glare at her. "I think Craig was the one messing with Iris's head."

She closes her eyes. "Fine." She turns off the engine and gets out with me. She tries to be polite. "Hello, Alex."

He stands up. "Mrs. Williams."

"Do y'all want to come inside? Where it's warm?" Mom says, unlocking the door. "I can make some hot chocolate." She's not really being hospitable. She wants us in the kitchen, where she can keep an eye on us.

"No, we'll just sit right here, Mom." I walk him over to the porch swing, giving her a smile.

She glares at me again and slams the door shut.

It's really not that cold.

Alex sits down on the porch swing with me. "I'm going to say I'm sorry one more time, but don't attack me."

I shake my head. "I shouldn't have done that. That was wrong of me."

He smiles, and it hurts my heart. "It's okay. I understand now how you felt. And I wanted to thank you for making me listen to you. I didn't deserve it."

"Yes, you did. Don't think for a minute that you deserve to be treated any other way, Alex."

His forehead wrinkles. I want to kiss his forehead until it's smooth and the weight of the world falls away from him. I want to hold his hand and squeeze it. I want to run my fingers through what's left of his hair.

I don't dare touch him, though.

"You're so different from her."

I am not expecting him to say this. And yet it's a cold and brutal truth. It's what I think I've been afraid of all along. That he still wants her and I am a poor substitute.

"But I don't think she was ever really the person I thought she was," he continues. "Obviously, she had her reasons, but the thing I think I mourn most about her death is the fact that I never got to really know Iris."

He's leaning forward with his elbows on his knees, slowly pushing us back and forth on the swing. He's fidgeting with his hands. Cracking his knuckles and twisting my nebula ring around on his pinkie finger. But he turns his head to look up at me. "Of course I was a different person back then too. I never bothered trying to get to know her any better. Never entertained the possibility that she was hurting inside and needed more than what I was offering."

I don't know if I want to hear this. This sounds too personal. Things Iris never shared with me, and didn't mention in her diary. But I remember Trista telling me Alex doesn't have anyone to open up with. There's nothing I can do but listen while my heart breaks silently.

"Anyway, I'm glad you're different." He looks away again, staring at the porch floor. "And I'm glad I'm a different person from who I was back then. I want to be the kind of person who deserves someone like you."

Wait. What? "Someone like me how?"

He looks back up at me. He reaches over and places his hand over mine, which has been gripping the edge of the seat. "Someone who's smart and kind and beautiful. Someone who knows what's going on in my head. Someone who's not afraid of my demons."

I flex my fingers so that his can slide in between mine. "I'm not afraid if you're not afraid," I whisper.

He pulls my hand away from the seat and turns it over, palm side up. He presses his lips against the heel of my hand and looks up at me with a wicked grin. "I'm terrified of you, Cupcake."

A trail of heat scorches from my hand up my arm and down my spine. But I want to laugh at his endearment.

I lean over and kiss him on the cheek. He smells like cedar and sage.

"I brought you this," he says, taking the nebula ring off his finger and sliding it on one of my own. "I finally figured out it must have been yours."

I smile. "It took you long enough." I wiggle my fingers and admire the pink and purple stardust of the Orion Nebula. I rest my head against his shoulder, happiness bubbling up inside my chest. Wait, I shouldn't feel this happy. Should I?

I know exactly how to ruin this perfect moment. "So my mom is planning on selling the house. She wants to move to Atlanta."

Alex nods carefully. "I can understand. She wants to make a clean start. That could be a good thing."

"But I want her to wait one more year, and let me finish high school," I say. "I don't want to lose my friends."

He's still holding my hand and gives it a squeeze. "You're not going to lose us. We'll be right here. Only an hour's drive away."

"If only I could drive." I start to pout.

"Well, I can drive. And I'll drive to your house every day to keep you from being lonely."

It's ridiculous, but it makes me feel better to imagine seeing him every day. "I'd like that. But maybe she'll change her mind. I hope I get to stay."

Alex smiles. "I hope so too. Otherwise I'd have to write poetry for some new mystery girl."

"That could be awkward," I say. "What if you wrote something like Pablo Neruda poetry on the desk and found out Hank sat in your seat in another period?"

He laughs at this, and I think how lucky I am to hear it. Somehow, we're both going to be okay.

"I know you were looking forward to being able to drive out and watch the Lyrid shower on your own, but would you mind some company? I happen to know a guy who has a driver's license and a truck for carting telescopes around."

Now I know Alex is too good to be true. My life is sup

posed to be a Greek tragedy, not a Disney fairy tale. Not that I'm complaining.

I'm just suspicious.

"Can this guy be trusted?" I ask. "If so, I can bring blankets and pillows and a thermos of hot cocoa."

"Just tell me where and when," Alex says, and his blue eyes twinkle when he smiles.

CHAPTER 30

Turns out the best spot for viewing a meteor shower within the city limits is the cemetery. But they lock the gates at five in the evening. Alex and I have a plan. And he has an uncle who works as a security guard. He's willing to let us in the cemetery after hours if Calcifer will play at his high school reunion next month.

Caleb should be out of jail by then. But Alex and Hank haven't decided if they're willing to keep him in the band.

Trista has agreed to let me "spend the night" with her on Friday.

Even though the Lyrids' peak night for viewing was on Thursday, we still hope for a good show Friday night. Of course Mom is home, not attending any builders convention now. But it's okay.

She knows about the meteor shower, and helps me pack the blankets and cocoa, and reminds me and Trista to bundle up warmly.

She wraps a fuchsia and purple scarf around my neck. "Have fun," she says.

Alex meets me at Trista's house, and we pack everything into his truck.

"You kids be careful out there," Trista says, her arms around Hank's waist.

Hank grins. "Don't forget the birth control."

Alex and I both blush as Trista slaps him on the arm. "Ignore him," she says as Alex opens the passenger door for me.

Hank's outburst causes an awkward silence as we drive across town.

"Did you finish a project for Verla's poetry fair?" I hate that I can't think of anything else to say.

Alex nods. "I needed the extra grade. It helped a lot."

"Which poet did you pick?"

His smile is shy, but he waggles his eyebrows. "Guess."

"You're so adorable. Give me a hint. What century?"

"Nineteenth."

"Male or female?"

"You only get one clue."

"Fine. Edgar Allan Poe."

"Nope." He pulls up to the entrance of the cemetery, just after sunset, and his uncle lets us through the gates. "You're going to have to tell me where to go," Alex tells me.

Oconee Hill stretches out over almost a hundred acres. The oldest graves in the front section date back to the eighteen hundreds. Iris is buried in one of the newer sections, across the river.

I haven't been back to see Iris since the funeral. Every time Mom came, I refused to accompany her. I was scared I would only remember her as lying in the ground. I want to remember her as she was, when she was alive.

Alex understands this. He missed the funeral, and, until now, hasn't had any desire to see her grave. I direct him across the narrow bridge and down winding lanes lined with headstones and ancient trees.

It's a beautiful and peaceful place.

He parks the truck along the side of the road, and I open my door. "Lord Byron," I say, guessing again. Alex Hammond is mad, bad, and dangerous indeed.

"Nope." Alex walks around to my side. He pins me against the door, his hands on my waist. I grab on to his shirt, and he bends his head down to mine. He hesitates, only for a moment, to give me a chance to push him away, but then his mouth meets mine and the world falls away.

His kisses are gentle, like a prayer, seeking and forgiving. The truck door is cold, but my heart is pounding and my skin is flushed. I don't mind the cold at all. All I know or feel or breathe is Alex.

"Robert Browning," I whisper against his lips.

"How did you guess?"

I push his sleeve back and slide my fingertips along his arm, where he's written in blue ink, *What matter to me if their star is a world? Mine has opened her soul to me; therefore I love her.*

I suck in a breath, remembering the lines in the book. "You changed a few words," I say.

Alex's only reply is another heart-stopping kiss. My arms twist around his neck, pulling my body closer to his.

His hands move up the sides of my rib cage, and my shirt rides up, exposing my belly to cold air. I gasp in shock, then giggle.

His lips pull away from mine. "Should we be doing this here?" But he's grinning.

I glance out behind him at the landscape. "I don't think anyone here minds."

He kisses me one more time, with more affection than heat, then drags me away from the truck. "Come on. We have stuff to do. Before we can do . . . more stuff."

I sigh. Stuff. I count rows back from the end of the road

and find the landmarks Mom had suggested. I shine the flashlight I've brought across the darkness. "See that river birch? And the pinkish-orange marble headstone right next to it?"

Alex looks where I'm pointing. "Yes. That's hers?"

"No, hers is the small gray one in front of that one."

There are still a few bouquets of silk flowers and a memorial wreath. I feel bad for not thinking to stop and pick up a rose before we came out here.

Alex stands next to me in front of the headstone. He reaches for my hand, and neither of us says anything for several minutes.

IRIS LYDIA WEBB

BELOVED DAUGHTER

1999–2015

The last dream I had of my sister, she was sitting in the kitchen, showing me postcards of my favorite astronomers. Carl Sagan. Caroline Herschel. Galileo. She was telling me how cool it was that she got to hang out with these people. In real life, Iris couldn't care less about dead astronomers. But I'd like to think the dream means something good. That she is somewhere much happier and she's finally found peace.

Alex bends down at a nearby grave and rights a small American flag that has been knocked over.

I slide the nebula ring off my finger and leave it on top of Iris's headstone. "Safe travels, Sis," I whisper.

There aren't a whole lot of trees in this section, so we set the blanket out at the end of Iris's row, where there are no graves yet. Besides the hot cocoa, we've brought a minicooler packed with sandwiches and binoculars.

It gets very dark fast. There are no street lights and there is no game tonight, so the nearby stadium is dark. I look up at the stars and gasp. I can see twice as many as I usually see from my backyard.

Alex pulls me down onto the blanket with him. "Are you cold?" he asks, as his arms wrap around me.

Blazing stars streak across the sky above us.

I shake my head. Love keeps me warm.

BEYOND THE BOOK

DISCUSSION QUESTIONS

1. Why does Andria identify with Antigone in the beginning of the story? Why does she grow to identify with a different character at the end?

2. Andria feels she can communicate better with Alex through poems written by other people. Can you think of any poems she might use to communicate anonymously with her friends? Her mom?

3. Have you ever sent a poem to someone anonymously? What was the poem?

4. If you had to create a project for the Poetry Fair, which poem would you choose? What do you think should be included on the project board?

5. Why did Andria feel overshadowed by her twin sister growing up? Does she still feel this way now that Iris is gone?

6. How does Andria's relationship with her mother change during the story? How does it stay the same?

Read on for an excerpt from Natalie's story,

The Form of Things Unknown,

coming September 2016 from Kensington.

Natalie Roman isn't much for the spotlight. But performing _A Midsummer Night's Dream_ in a stately old theater in Savannah, Georgia, beats sitting alone replaying mistakes made in Athens. Fairy queens and magic on stage, maybe a few scary stories backstage. And no one in the cast knows her backstory.

Except for Lucas—he was in the psych ward, too. He won't even meet her eye. But Nat doesn't need him. She's making friends with girls, girls who like horror movies and Ouija boards, who can hide their liquor in Coke bottles and laugh at the theater's ghosts. Natalie can keep up. She can adapt. And if she skips her meds once or twice so they don't interfere with her partying, it won't be a problem. She just needs to keep her wits about her.

Honest, nuanced, and bittersweet, _The Form of Things Unknown_ explores the shadows that haunt even the truest hearts . . . and the sparks that set them free.

The lunatic, the lover and the poet
Are of imagination all compact:
One sees more devils than vast hell can hold,
That is, the madman: the lover, all as frantic,
Sees Helen's beauty in a brow of Egypt:
The poet's eye, in fine frenzy rolling,
Doth glance from heaven to earth, from earth to heaven;
And as imagination bodies forth
The forms of things unknown, the poet's pen
Turns them to shapes and gives to airy nothing
A local habitation and a name.

—Theseus, *A Midsummer Night's Dream,* act 5, scene 1

CHAPTER 1

The course of true love never did run smooth.
—A Midsummer Night's Dream, act 1, scene 1

My grandmother is listening to the Beatles again. Loudly. She refuses to use earbuds because she says bugs can crawl out of the tiny speakers and into your brain that way. John Lennon's voice travels up the stairs and under the doors and through the thin walls of this smelly old house. Lennon's lyrics reach me all the way up here in the attic, where my parents have cleared a space for my mattress and a small bookshelf for my sketch pads. *Your castle in the sky,* my mother joked. *I'm the madwoman in the attic,* I joked back.

Mom didn't laugh.

Grandma particularly loves "Strawberry Fields." She says the angels talk to her through this song. And I worry that the longer I lie here and listen, I'm going to hear the angels talking to me too.

My brother doesn't think I'm crazy. At least he doesn't treat me like a crazy person, and I'm grateful for that. Ever since I was discharged from Winter Oaks, rated the best adolescent psych unit in eastern Georgia, Mom and Dad have hovered over me, watching me like a ticking time bomb.

They make sure I take my pills, and ask me a million times a day if I'm feeling all right. How should I feel? I'm curled up in my bed under my quilt, even though the attic is hot and stuffy, and I wonder if I can even describe the sensations I'm feeling. I can't call them emotions. At least not right now. There are only a million thoughts. Emotionless thoughts buzzing around my head like insects.

Thankfully, my parents now have Grandma to worry about. Maybe they'll forget to worry about me. Until I do something terrible. Something crazy.

"Hey, Hippie." David tromps up the stairs and knocks on the door as he's pushing it open.

"What's up, Hick?" I don't bother to raise my head from the pillow.

He plops himself down next to me. Grandma's ancient calico cat has been cuddled up against me all morning. Now she hisses at David and jumps down. "Nat, I need a favor."

"From *moi?* I have no money."

I've been meaning to look for a summer job, but Dad hasn't pushed the issue, so I really haven't looked that hard.

My brother picks up the nearest stuffed animal, the phallic-looking naked mole rat from *Kim Possible,* and starts tossing it up in the air, catching it like a football. "Do you know anything about the theater workshop they're doing this summer downtown?"

I try to grab Rufus away from him, but David keeps the naked mole rat out of my reach. "Um, I think they're doing *A Midsummer Night's Dream.*"

"I was thinking about trying out. Want to come with me?"

I stare at my brother, with his backward baseball cap. "Are you feeling okay?"

"I'm just looking for something to do this summer. I figured you knew all about that hippie drama stuff, so . . ." I think he is actually blushing.

Now I sit straight up as I continue to stare him down. "Since when were you into hippie drama stuff?" My brother is not really a hick. Far from it, actually. But he dresses like one and drives a monster truck that I tease him about mercilessly.

"All right," he says, setting the naked mole rat down. "You know Colton, who works at the Pirate House?"

My jaw drops. "You've got to be kidding. You two are like night and day! He's, like, a goth queen!"

David has been trying to get me out of the house this summer, dragging me to his favorite coffeehouse in the city. I know I should be grateful to have a big brother who isn't afraid to let his little sister tag along with him, and I do like to sit and people watch at the coffeehouse. And the café is next door to a wonderfully seedy-looking comic book store. One day I'm going to get up the nerve to go in there.

"He sat in front of me in Composition last semester," David says. "He'd draw these funny little pictures on my notebooks."

"Is that why you failed that course? Are you saying it was the Queen of the Night's fault?" David just barely squeaked by his freshman year at the Savannah College of Art and Design, affectionately known as SCAD. My brother is majoring in architecture.

"No, but that's why I need your help. My English professor is directing the play. She'll kick me out of the theater for sure unless you come to tryouts with me."

"Me? Just because you got a bad grade in Comp One doesn't mean she won't let you work on the play. Besides, why would I want to go to play tryouts? I'm the antisocial one, remember?"

"Because you love your brother more than anyone else in the world." David sighs and fidgets with his cap. "I need you to come with me so I won't look like a theater dork. I'll just be there for my little hippie sister who can't drive yet."

He ducks as I throw Rufus at his head. "It's not like you have anything else to do this summer besides hide from the sun and sew weird clothes. Here's your chance to wear weird clothes on stage. If you don't want to try out for a part, maybe you could just work on costumes."

"Ooh, fairy dresses." I could have fun with this. Possibly. Except I really can't sew that well yet.

"And you don't want me to tell Dad about you climbing out your window and sneaking off to that bonfire with your weird friends."

I sit straight up in my bed. "How do you know about that? You weren't even in Athens at the time." If I hadn't snuck out that night with Caleb, I probably wouldn't have ended up in Winter Oaks.

David rolls his eyes. "I'm the big brother. I know more about sneaking out than you. So, are you coming?"

He does not know everything about my bonfire story. If he did, he'd know what Caleb did that night, and David wouldn't ask me to help set him up with anyone like Colton. Straight or otherwise, bad boys really can be bad for you.

Still, the theater workshop sounds interesting. And even though I've never been in a play before, I do love Shakespeare. Even madwomen have to leave their attics sometimes.

"When are tryouts?" I finally ask.

My brother grins. He knows he's got me. "Tomorrow at three."

"Tomorrow?" What am I going to wear? My stomach starts hurting already.

"You'll do great, I know it." David pats me on the knee, then jumps up before I can hit him with the naked mole rat again.

I flop back on my bed, listening to him stomp down the
stairs and out the door, back to his dorm. I missed him so much
when he left for college last year, and we still lived in Athens.
But Mom and Dad and I had to move to Savannah last month
to be here with Grandma after Grandpa died. She refuses to
take her psych meds anymore, and before Grandpa was even
buried, the cops had already called Dad, when they found
Grandma trying to set the house on fire.

She claims she was cold and thought she was lighting the
fireplace. Why she thought she needed a fire in the middle of
May, I can't understand. It's extra hot up here in the attic, and
even though Dad promises to get me a small window-unit air
conditioner, it's not on the top of his list of priorities right
now.

My parents are under way too much stress this summer.
Dealing with Grandpa's death, and Grandma's craziness, and all
of this happening right after my misadventure.

I pull my damp hair off the back of my neck and stare up
at the ceiling. George Harrison is singing now. A slow, sad song
about his weeping guitar. Grandma prefers the later Beatles al-
bums to their earlier work. The long-haired hippie years. Dad
is constantly throwing away her incense so she won't set the
house on fire again.

I know it's too hot up here to light any incense, but it
would certainly help to disguise the cat litter smell that per-
meates the whole house.

No, I can't hide up here in this attic all summer long. I have
to get out and do something. If I have to try out for a play in
front of a bunch of strangers, that's okay. David will be there.
And maybe I can help him win the love of his life.

CHAPTER 2

The old Savannah Theater is in one of the revitalized areas of downtown. Built back in the eighteen hundreds, according to Mrs. Green, it was closed for almost fifty years until a community arts group begged some money from local businesses and got some state grants last year. The dragon lady, as David calls her, introduces herself and welcomes us to the Savannah Theater Summer Workshop. She is a tiny woman, dressed in a dark purple sundress, with short spiky silvery hair. She gestures grandly with elegant long arms as she tells us about the historical theater.

Mrs. Green is particularly proud of the new lighting system they installed in March. What they need next, I think, as I look around the dingy theater, are some new stage curtains. The burgundy velvet drapes are looking pretty grim.

Still, I love the ornate molding that decorates the walls and frames the stage. I can imagine this was a beautiful place back in its day. I glance around at the various clusters of kids sitting in the rows of seats. A group of little girls sit in the very front, chatting and flipping their ponytails back and forth. Their leader blows bubbles with her gum and looks very bored.

Up on the stage, a group of silly boys are practicing stage falls. Not that anyone would need to be doing stage falls in *A Midsummer Night's Dream*. A pretty brunette is laughing at them and practicing her English accent. "I say! Thou art too funny, y'all!"

Over by the little girls, I notice a baseball cap. Someone is wearing a baseball cap INSIDE THE THEATER. And Mrs. Green is saying nothing about it. Even David has taken off his cap. The boy sits reading, oblivious to everything going on around him. And I realize I know Baseball Cap Boy. It's Lucas . . . Something. Crap, did I know he lived in Savannah? I can't remember.

Lucas was a patient at Winter Oaks while I was there. We had a few group circles together. He's quiet and, from what I remember, a preacher's son. Lucas Grant. He was battling depression. And . . . a suicide attempt, I think.

"Hippie," David says, pinching my arm. "Let's sit over there." He nods toward the middle of the auditorium, where Colton and two girls are sitting. One of them has long black hair streaked with deep blue. She is intimidatingly beautiful. She glances up at us when Colton waves, and looks right back down at her phone.

I wave to the other girl, recognizing her from the counter at the Pirate House. Her pale blond hair has purple streaks. Starla smiles and waves back at me. Good. I won't be too scared to sit with this group.

I miss my friends in Athens terribly. But I don't miss Caleb. And I don't think I could go back to high school there, where everyone knows what happened to me. So in a way, I'm kind of glad Grandma had her psychotic episode and we had to move to Savannah. Thank you, Grandma.

From the other side of the aisle, Lucas glances my way, frowns, and turns back to his book.

Fine. I can pretend I don't know you either, Ass Hat.

"David!" Colton squeals. "What's up, baby?" We drop into the seats right behind them.

To his credit, my brother doesn't bat an eyelash. "I had no idea you guys would be here. This is great."

To my credit, I don't snort at this blatant lie. At least, I try not to. Blue-hair Girl looks at me as I try to choke back a giggle. "Are you David's sister?" she asks. "Are you trying out for the play? I think you'd make a great fairy queen. Your hair is gorgeous."

I can't help but blush. I've always hated my red curls. They never behave like I want them to, no matter what beauty products I buy or which salon I go to. I have hopeless hair. Not gorgeous hair.

"Raine, this is Natalie," Starla says, introducing us. I give her a grateful smile. "She's right, Nat. You could be Titania!"

I think I blush again. "I don't know if I could handle a big part like that. I'm really more interested in working on the costumes."

Starla rolls her eyes. "You're too nice, honey. If you want to be an actress, you're going to have to be much more aggressive."

Do I want to be an actress? I haven't given it much thought beyond this summer play thing. Starla seems dead serious in her ambition. She is looking up at the ceiling, inspecting the new lighting system. "My pale skin tends to look better under warm-colored gels. I hope they don't use the blue lights on me."

"You just need to get out into the sun more," Raine says. She is inspecting the ceiling too. A plaster medallion decorated with frolicking cherubs floats precariously above our heads. "I heard this theater is haunted," she says. "I wonder if we'll see any ghosts."

Before I can ask what she means by this, Mrs. Green walks onto the stage with a clipboard and makes some announcements about the summer production. "Cell phones off, children. For the first group, let's get Colton Barnes, Starla Hayes, and Natalie Roman up here," Mrs. Green says. "Let's see what you've got, people. Start on page five. And remember to speak loudly and clearly!"

But wait, I didn't put my name down for the auditions. Did I? I open my mouth to protest, to say that's not why I'm here. But I'm paralyzed.

David pats me on the knee. "Just go ahead and try it. You'll do great."

Starla smiles at me as she stands up, but it's not a friendly smile. "We're up!"

I don't want to disappoint anyone. I don't smile back as I stand up. I'm too nervous.

I pray my stomach will unknot itself by the time I walk to the front of the auditorium. I pray that I won't do anything stupid, like trip up the stairs.

I haven't been on a stage since kindergarten, when our class performed *The Food Pyramid*. (I was the celery.) The stage lights aren't on, so I can see everyone's faces in the audience. David sticks his tongue out at me.

I tell myself, this is Shakespeare. You love old poetry. You can do this. And if not, what's the worst that can happen? No one will die, right?

Of course not, Nat.

And I do okay. Not that I think it's an Academy Award–winning performance, but I make it through my lines without stumbling and without Mrs. Green having to yell "Louder!" more than once. I even glance up from the script once or twice to look at Starla while I'm reading and gesture with my hand. I hope I get bonus points for the gesturing.

Starla gets points docked for not spitting her gum out.

Colton grins at me flirtatiously. He is a beautiful boy with short black hair and black as night eyes, rimmed with just a hint of eyeliner. He reads well, too, with a wicked English accent.

"Good job, people," Mrs. Green says. "Next up, let me see

Ferris and Raine." Raine smiles nervously at me as I pass her
in the aisle. "Y'all did great!" she whispers.

"Thanks, good luck!" I tell her as I sit back down next to
my brother. I'm so glad it's over.

"You did great, Colton," he says, ignoring me.

David reads next, with a few of the little girls I saw hanging out near Lucas. The little divas can act rings around my
brother, but he does okay. He sits down on the end of the row
next to me, as Mrs. Green calls the next group up.

"Would someone be a dear and go get me a Coke?" Colton
pulls a dollar out of his wallet and waves it in the air. "My throat
is so dry now."

"Sure," my brother says, hopping up. "Put your money
away. I got it."

"My throat's dry too," I say.

David looks at me and rolls his eyes. "All right. Be right
back."

Starla giggles at me when he leaves. "Your brother's cute."

Colton is watching David's . . . ass? Even though he doesn't
say anything, I think that's a good sign.

I don't know if I should tell Starla that she's not David's
type. "Yeah? I suppose." My brother would make a wonderful
gypsy, with his long red curls that he usually keeps pulled back
under a Braves cap. He has only the tiniest hint of a goatee. So
not the image of your average truck-driving hick. He broke so
many girls' hearts in high school.

A cold draft blows through the theater, as if the air-
conditioning has just kicked on.

"Hey," David says, handing us our Cokes. I would have
preferred a Dr. Pepper, but I keep quiet.

"Thanks, sweetie," Colton says. I hope he really does like
my brother. I would hate to think I was doing all this for no
reason.

David and Colton begin chatting like long-lost friends,

and since Raine and Starla have their heads together plotting to take over the world for all I know, I try to watch what's going on up on the stage. But my mind must be bored.

It starts working in overdrive.

Those kids up on stage are really good. I don't think my audition was that strong, after all. The girl with the black ponytail uses an English accent and seems to be perfectly comfortable with iambic pentameter. The guy reading for Bottom actually juggles.

I can't compete with a juggler.

And I'm nowhere near as cute as the little five-year-olds. Maybe I should have worn fairy wings today.

I let out a breath and see Raine and Starla glance back at me.

They're whispering about my sucktastic audition.

My heart starts getting wound up, and my hands begin to sweat. Oh no. I'm overcome with a sudden sense of impending doom and must escape. Somewhere in the back of my brain, I think I know I'm having a panic attack, but the rest of my brain is in FLEE FOR YOUR LIFE mode. I stand up, grabbing David by the shoulder.

"Be back in a minute," I mutter, before climbing out into the aisle.

"'K." He doesn't even look up at me. He doesn't care anymore. He probably wants me to leave him and Colton alone anyway.

I try not to stumble as I walk up the aisle toward the exit. Everyone is watching me, I can feel their stares on me. Ugh.

I open the doors as quietly as possible, but light from the foyer still floods the darkened auditorium. Draw even more attention to yourself, Nat.

The women's bathroom off the foyer has a sign on the door: UNDER CONSTRUCTION, PARDON OUR MESS! I'm not about to use the men's room, so I head toward the backstage area, hunting for the dressing rooms.

It's quiet back here. All the lights are off, so I move slowly with my phone out for a little bit of light.

It's actually too quiet. My ears begin to buzz. I feel relief when I see the women's dressing room door and push it open, making a slight squeak.

There are several toilet stalls and even two shower stalls back here. Good to know, I guess. I'm not in any hurry to get back to that crowd, but I would hate for David to say something smart ass about me falling in.

I head back through the dark backstage area and see the back row of curtains move. The area grows chilly around me, and in the dim light I think I see a person standing there, looking at me.

I don't know if it's someone auditioning or someone working here at the theater. "Sorry!" I say. "Just had to use the bathroom!"

The person doesn't say anything, and I hurry past, anxious now to be back in my seat next to my brother.

I turn around just as I open the door to the hallway, but the person in the shadows is gone.

At the end of tryouts, Mrs. Green announces that she'll be making final decisions within the next two days. Practice will be from five to eight, Monday through Friday, with set work days on the weekends. The performance will be in four weeks.

I feel a nervous little jiggle in my stomach. What am I doing here? Performances? In front of people? I lean over and whisper to David, "Maybe this isn't such a hot idea." I could be spending my summer at the beach instead of stuck in this moldy old theater.

"Don't give up now, or I'll have to tell Mom and Dad about the bonfire with Caleb."

I hate my brother.

As we stand up to leave, I tug on David's arm. "Look up there on the stage. Do you see the curtains moving? There was someone back there when I went looking for the bathroom."

"Where?" David asks.

"The curtains in the back. See how they're swaying?"

David takes a look onstage and frowns. "What are you talking about?"

"You don't see the curtains moving up there?"

He stares at the stage again. Then looks back at me. "Oh, Nat." My brother sighs heavily, and glances around to see if anyone else is nearby, listening. "Not again."

CHAPTER 3

I look at my brother and get a sick feeling in my stomach. My gaze swings from his sad face back up to the stage. The curtains my brother can't see. Crap. Why did I say anything?

David has his hand on my shoulder. "It's okay, Nat. Did you—"

"Of course I took my meds!" I whisper. No one is paying attention to us, though. Starla is playing with Colton's phone, listening to his music with earbuds in. Raine is talking with Mrs. Green up onstage.

"All right. Maybe I just didn't look fast enough."

"Whatever. Can we go home?" I don't want to be here anymore. It must be the stress from auditioning. If I was hallucinating about the curtains, maybe the person backstage wasn't real either.

"Colton asked if we wanted to stop at the sushi place down the street. I know you like their soup."

I sigh. I really don't feel like hanging out with strangers right now. Getting to know new people and trying to keep them from learning you're a freak is exhausting. "Why don't you go without me? You'd probably make a better impression solo."

David looks concerned. "No, if you want to go home, I'll take you home. We'll tell them you have a migraine or something."

And he lies so beautifully, I think he'll make a wonderful Shakespearean actor. I manage a feeble smile at Starla when she and Raine tell me they hope I feel better soon.

Colton pouts. "We'll miss you two." But he's looking at David when he says this.

"See, I'm helping you play hard to get," I tell my brother, when we are in the truck driving back to Grandma's.

He grins. "I already got his phone number."

"David!"

"But I want to hear more about you. Did you meet any hot boys in the psych unit last month?"

I roll my eyes. And the image of Lucas in the theater flashes before my eyes. He is so not my type.

"Who's not your type?"

Crap. Was I talking out loud? "Um, there was a boy at Winter Oaks that I saw at the theater today. But really, he's not my type."

David glances over at me, his pierced eyebrow cocked up. "Sis, the last boy you dated went to jail for dealing drugs. Before that, the other one slept with half of your class. While the two of you were going out. Maybe you need a new type."

I shake my head. "I don't think hooking up with a fellow psych patient is a smart idea."

"Probably not." He shrugs. "But tell me about this crazy but hot boy you met."

I love my brother to death. "I don't really know much about him. He was at Winter Oaks for a suicide attempt, I think, though he kept telling the counselors it was an accident. Obviously they didn't believe him, or he wouldn't have been there, right?"

"Hmm. Cute?"

"*You'd* think he was." Lucas has floppy blond hair that usually hangs over his face. When it's not hiding under a baseball cap. "Dresses like he belongs on the CW."

David's second "Hmm" goes up an octave.

"Oh, but he definitely doesn't swing for your team. I just remembered the reason he tried to kill himself was because of his girlfriend dumping him. So he's not the boy for you, and definitely not for me. Don't need someone that hung up on an ex."

"But you just said he claimed he didn't try to kill himself."

"He overdosed on sleeping pills and alcohol."

"Did he leave a note?"

I shrug. I guess I shouldn't make any judgments when I've never held a conversation with Lucas before. But as I don't have any plans to have any deep conversations with him at the theater, it doesn't matter. And really, I don't think he's cute.

Much.